The Final Ritual

Truth can be subjective, manipulated or even wrong.

Arsalaan Javed

Disclaimer

Acknowledgment

This is my first novel, and it has been a journey filled with challenges and rewards. This wouldn't be possible without the support of amazing people in my life.

First and foremost, I would like to thank my parents Mr. Javed Shaukat and Mrs. Shaheen Javed who showered their love and prayers upon me all through my life. My brothers, Amaan Javed and Nomaan Javed Khan, who have constantly been the pillars of my strength, challenging and supporting me to become a better self.

Finally, I am eternally thankful to my wife Areeba Fatima, who has shown unbroken faith in me and supported me throughout my journey of writing this book and helped me to review this book.

Table of Contents

Chapter 1:
The crime scene

Looking through a double-layered insulated window, one can easily see a leafless tree with its branches covered with snow and reflecting a dim white light from the sky, contrasting with the warm glow of street lamps. The scene evokes the atmosphere of an ancient oil painting adorning the wall of this Montreal apartment on a cold night. Detective Marc Blanc and his assistant, Aynaz, arrive at the crime scene on Ridgewood Avenue in Cote-Des-Neiges around 7 p.m. on March 17th. Recent heavy snowfall has blanketed the city, leaving frozen peaks on rooftops, damp streets, and snowy walkways.

The first to arrive at the apartment is Sajid Khan, the victim's father. A man of average height for an Indian, Sajid, in his sixties, sports a balding head with white-gray hair at the sides. He was wearing a traditional Indian kurta pajama in a dark coffee color, which seemed out of place in the frigid Canadian weather. His forehead had a darkened patch, a mark of his devotion to the Muslim faith. His eyes were filled with tears, and he had a running nose and trembling lips.

Sajid is accompanied by his wife, Najma Begum, who clings to him, her sobs reverberating through the apartment. Dressed in a traditional white Salwar and Kurta, her head is covered with a white dupatta, and the jangling of her golden bangles is a stark reminder of the joyous occasions they were meant for. She was howling and crying, holding Sajid's hand in that apartment.

As Marc enters the apartment, his gray eyes scan the surroundings. Appointed as the lead investigating officer, he is a Canadian police detective born, raised, and residing in Quebec his entire life. Primarily a francophone, he has also mastered English for interrogations and investigations. Tall and solidly built with a hint of gray in his hair, he maintains a healthy physique despite his smoking habit. He wears a long black overcoat over a fleece sweater and gray trousers. Known for his keen observation and investigation skills, he is well-suited for this homicide case in Montreal.

The apartment was a modest one-bedroom, painted white on the walls and brightly lit, making it easily visible from outside. Upon entering, a short passage led to a washroom on the left, which appeared unremarkable upon inspection. A small closet for overcoats and boots sat opposite the washroom, containing only a men's winter boot of size twelve.

The wooden floor creaked underfoot as he moved further into the apartment. He entered a small hall with a two-seater sofa facing a large television near a big window overlooking the street. To the left of the hall was an open kitchen, where an unopened food parcel from Hero Burger restaurant sat on the kitchen slab. Adjacent to the kitchen was a bedroom featuring a queen-sized bed with a rumpled bed sheet and an unmade quilt, suggesting prolonged occupancy. A water humidifier emitted a lavender fragrance from the bedside table, while a collage of pictures adorned one wall, depicting Maysa with friends, family, and childhood memories.

In the center of the hall, a four-chaired white round dining table held a grim sight, a lifeless body. Maysa's head rested on the table top, her hands covered in spilled tea, and a white teacup was overturned with lip gloss marks. Despite the tragic scene, her face holds a calm, peaceful expression as if she was free now.

Maysa, just shy of her 28th birthday, wore a white cotton T-shirt and blue woolen joggers. Her brownish-dyed hair fell into medium to long strands. Slim and fit at 5'4", she bore distinctive features reminiscent of her Indian Muslim heritage, including a sharp nose, curled eyelashes, and tidy eyebrows.

Antoine, a young, tall, and well-built police officer, was the first reporting officer to arrive at the crime scene. The call came in around 6:15 PM from Sajid, prompting Antoine's swift response, reaching the scene by 6:30 PM. Upon arrival, he found Sajid and Najma distraught, holding their daughter and crying. Antoine immediately instructed them to step aside from the body, preserving the crime scene's integrity. He obtained statements from the parents and directed them to the police station for further assistance.

Approaching Marc upon his arrival, Antoine reported, "There was no sign of forced entry, Sir. The door was locked from the inside, as confirmed by the father. They had to use a key to gain entry when there was no response to their calls or doorbells. We found an unwashed utensil in the sink, suggesting recent use, along with a food parcel on the kitchen slab. There are no apparent signs of a struggle or forced entry, indicating a possible suicide. However, we did observe an 11-foot-size shoe mark outside the apartment, likely belonging to a delivery person. Sajid mentioned finding the food parcel outside the door upon his arrival."

Antoine omitted the detail about Sajid and Najma holding their daughter upon his arrival, possibly to spare them further distress on the day of their loss.

Marc acknowledged Antoine's report with a nod, remaining silent as he processed the information.

Marc approached Sajid, his French-English accent evident as he inquired, "Why were you here?" After briefly pausing, he added, "Don't you have a restaurant? You should have been busy since it's a holiday today."

Still visibly upset and dabbing at his eyes and nose with a tissue, Sajid was surprised that Marc already knew about his profession. He explained, "Yes, we were just dropping off Roohi, our second daughter, to Maysa, as we usually do, when Najma needed to assist me with the restaurant work."

"And where is she?" Marc asked.

"We left her in the car outside. We didn't want these images to haunt her for the rest of her life," Sajid replied.

Marc noted that Antoine had omitted details about the second daughter, or perhaps he had never inquired about her.

Deciding not to press further, Marc instructed everyone to vacate the crime scene. He then proceeded to the bedroom, where he found another door leading to the balcony. Although it was winter, the balcony door was not locked. Marc ventured outside and observed that the balcony was not too high from the ground, making it a potential escape route.

Returning to the hall, Marc stood near Maysa's body, imagining the view she would have had from her position. He noted that the entire apartment was visible, and a sneak attack from behind would have been impossible due to the wall behind her. Additionally, the lack of drapes allowed visibility into the apartment from the road and the building across the street, ruling out the possibility of forced entry or a struggle within the apartment.

Marc pondered why Maysa would sit in the innermost chair of the table unless someone else was already seated at the open end. However, he found only one cup on the table, with no other signs of company.

Approaching the table, Marc examined the plain white teacup before heading to the kitchen to search for clues. Finding nothing suspicious except an unwashed utensil in the sink and an unopened food parcel on the counter, he questioned why Maysa would order food or prepare tea if she were planning to commit suicide.

Convinced in his mind that it was a murder, likely by poison and by someone known to Maysa due to the lack of forced entry or struggle, Marc sought to determine if the killer was present in the apartment at the time of her death or if the poisoning was premeditated.

Turning to Aynaz, Marc inquired about Indian tea cup traditions, leading to a brief discussion about tea cup sets and designs. With a sense of acknowledgment, Marc concluded it was a cold-blooded murder and that the killer was present in the apartment.

Antoine and Aynaz were astonished by Marc's conclusion, while Sajid and Nagma were shocked upon hearing the news. Antoine questioned Marc's certainty, seeking clarification.

Marc responded, "I found only 4 of these cups from the set in the kitchen and one on the table. So, either the sixth cup was broken before, but given it is a new set of teacups and the other four cups are still in their packaging, it is less probable. Or the sixth cup was taken by the murderer, fearing he or she would have left a fingerprint on it."

Locking eyes with Marc, Aynaz asked, "How do you conclude that?"

Marc elaborated, "Well, from the way she was sitting. If she was alone, she would have sat at the open end of the table or maybe on the sofa set. But she chose to sit in the inner chair, which people only do when other seats are already occupied. Additionally, this apartment is brightly lit, and the drapes are undone, so it would be visible from outside. Thus, no one could have tried to tangle or force her. Most likely, she consumed the poison from her drink. The forensic report will confirm this. And finally, there is no suicide note present. From my experience, people mostly write a final note to their loved ones before they take their life."

An announcement interrupted their conversation, stating that the forensic team had arrived, and everyone needed to vacate the premises for evidence collection.

Marc turned to Antoine and instructed, "Did you take a statement from Roohi, her sister?"

Surprised that he might have missed a crucial step, Antoine replied, "No, Sir."

Marc continued, "Please get her statement. Also, take this parcel and go to the restaurant to confirm who placed the order and when it was placed."

Turning to Aynaz, Marc requested, "Can you ask officers to canvass the neighborhood for any suspicious activity today? And inquire with the apartment below if they heard any sounds around 5:30 - 6:30 pm. This floor makes a squeaky sound; they would have heard it if there were any movements."

Aynaz added, "Sure, Marc. One more thing, Maysa is missing a nail. This could be from before as well."

Marc examined Maysa's missing nail and instructed, "Good observation. Let the forensic team know so they can search the apartment for it. Maybe we'll get a DNA match. Also, ask the Khans to come to the police station for a formal statement and to bring their second daughter."

As Antoine left, he informed Marc, "We found a mobile phone in the bedroom. There were four missed calls from Sajid around 6 PM, one call from James at 4 PM, one from Hina at noon, and some text messages exchanged with Rehan this morning."

Marc, pleased with the additional evidence, instructed Antoine to confiscate the phone and send it to the team for analysis.

He departed the premises with Aynaz by his side.

Chapter 2:
First information report

Around 8:00 PM on the same day of the murder, Marc arrived at the police station on Saint Catherine Street in Downtown Montreal with the rest of Sajid's family and Aynaz. Marc instructed Aynaz to take Sajid and Najma to his office. A slight sense of compassion for the family stirred within Aynaz, as she, too, was Indian.

Aynaz had reservations about bringing the grieving family to the police station. "Is it necessary to question them today? You also asked to bring their younger daughter," she voiced her concerns.

"I understand your sympathy, but trust me, the only thing that can give them relief now is knowing who killed their daughter. Moreover, the sooner we start, the better. Suspects tend to make mistakes initially, but if we wait too long, they may normalize the situation and calm themselves, making it harder to differentiate them," Marc explained.

Accepting his reasoning, Aynaz nodded and followed his orders, leaving Sajid and Najma in the office. Taking Roohi with her, she instructed, "Please wait here. If you need anything, please let me know."

Completely exhausted from sobbing, Sajid asked, "When can

we get our daughter's body for her final rituals?"

Aynaz responded gently, "Normally, the medical examiner takes around 24 hours to release the body. I will inform you as soon as it is available for you to take."

As talk of their daughter as an object brought Najma to tears again, Aynaz silently understood her emotions and led Roohi out of the room.

At 8:15 PM, Marc entered his office, a small, beige-colored room cluttered with documents. A large wooden table dominated the center, papers spread across its surface. One side of the table held an office chair with lumbar support, where Marc sat, while the other accommodated two small chairs for Sajid and Najma.

Marc softly addressed Sajid, "I am sorry to bring you directly to the station. I can understand that you must be in so much pain." His tone hardened as he continued, "The sooner we start our investigation, the sooner we will be able to catch the murderer here, and I know you must want the same thing, don't you?"

Sajid, sensing suspicion, nodded in response.

Aynaz re-entered the room, announcing, "Roohi is with Antoine." She pulled in an extra chair and positioned it beside Marc, ready to take notes.

Marc then turned his attention to Sajid and Najma. "Not to worry, this is not an interrogation. I just want to gather some details about Maysa before we can begin our investigation and file the initial information report."

Focusing on Najma, Marc asked, "Can you tell me something about Maysa?"

Najma, surprised by the sudden request, hesitated before composing herself. "She was a very nice person, kind at heart, and she loved us a lot. She used to visit us as often as possible, spending time with Roohi and us. She helped Roohi with her homework and spent hours talking to her. Maysa was ambitious and smart, always at the top of her class, and nice to everyone. Even at her job, she received an appraisal recently and immediately called us to share the news. She had the opportunity to join a multinational company outside of Montreal but chose to stay closer to us."

As Najma recounted memories of her daughter, she became emotional, recalling Maysa's determination and achievements. "I still remember when she was around thirteen years old," Najma continued, wiping away tears. "She participated in a literature competition against her sister Hina. Though she initially lost, Maysa worked tirelessly for the next round, ultimately emerging as the first-place winner."

Sajid noticed Aynaz scribbling something on her pad, and Marc observed Sajid's gaze.

Interrupting Najma, Marc turned to Sajid. "Can you add any other details about her?"

Sajid responded, "I can't even express how wonderful she was to us. She used to call us every day."

Marc interjected, "But she didn't call you today?"

Remaining composed, Sajid replied, "Yes, today we were supposed to be busy with our restaurant as it is St. Patrick's Day today, and we were completely booked."

Marc remained silent, his gaze fixed on Sajid.

Sajid continued, "She was a very friendly person and had many friends, but she was closest to Hina, her cousin, and Tracey, her childhood friend. The three of them were inseparable and shared everything. Maysa had a way of bringing out the best in people, which made her well-liked."

Aynaz jotted down notes once more.

Sajid continued, "She was born in India, but we moved to Canada when she was only one year old. She had her primary education in Montreal and was fluent in both French and English, which helped us settle in Quebec. As Najma mentioned, she excelled in her studies. She completed her undergraduate at McGill University and became a computer software engineer. Five years ago, she co-founded her own company specializing in converting speech to text, text to data, and data to information. This information was used to provide better product recommendations to clients."

Marc inquired, "Is there anything else coming to your mind now?"

Sajid added, "Yes, she didn't start her company alone. She co-founded it with Andre Baudelaire, whom she met while studying at McGill University. The company has thrived, especially in the last 3 years, employing over 50 people and serving clients globally."

Marc prompted, "Do you want to tell us anything else about her?"

Sajid replied, "I have mostly shared what comes to mind."

"Thank you for providing these details about Maysa," Marc acknowledged. "You mentioned moving to Canada when she was only a year old. Can you explain why you made that decision with an infant?

Sajid took a deep breath before explaining, "Actually, no one wants to leave their home country and immigrate to another country without a reason. In the late nineties, during an economic crisis, I lost my job shortly after getting married. Despite trying odd jobs, I wasn't making enough to provide a decent life for my family. I wanted to raise my child in a better environment, with access to quality education."

Marc nodded in understanding. "Certainly. Can you tell me about yourself and your work here?"

Sajid replied, "As you know, we own Desi Pakwan, a fine-dining Indian restaurant downtown. Thankfully, it's doing well."

Marc remarked, "I've heard it's one of the best. You must be quite well-off?"

Sajid replied modestly, "I wouldn't say rich, but we're doing alright, thanks to God's grace."

Marc glanced at Aynaz, jesting, "If having a house in Westmount is just doing alright, then sign me up."

Turning back to Sajid, Marc inquired, "Can you tell us more about yourself and your beliefs?"

Hinting what he wanted to know, Sajid responded, "I am a practicing Muslim. I pray to God five times a day, and I go to the mosque regularly. I am also an active member of the Muslim community in Montreal, and I take pride in doing so because we help the needy and poor and spread peace and harmony among each other."

Marc clarified, "I'm not trying to offend you. I am just seeking insight. Was Maysa also practicing Islam?"

Sajid admitted, "She followed teachings in her childhood but strayed as she grew older. She practiced, but not fully."

With a stern tone, Marc pressed, "By not fully, do you mean having a non-Muslim boyfriend? Why hide her relationship with James Clove? Were you unaware?"

Sajid felt embarrassed either because his daughter had a relationship with a non-Muslim or maybe because he hid this fact about her, as he never approved of this relationship. He admitted, "Yes, he was her boyfriend. But she didn't love him; he had somehow influenced her to become his girlfriend."

Aynaz thought to herself with a smirk, "A typical Indian man's behavior regarding his daughter's boyfriend."

Marc inquired, "Can you please tell us something about James?"

Sajid responded angrily, "He is a theater actor, and he is about the same age as Maysa. He came into my daughter's life for her money, as he wasn't rich or had decent earnings. They met around three years ago, and after that, my daughter changed. He was a bad influence on her. He even tricked her into drinking alcohol and smoking weed, which is not allowed in our religion. She was caught in a drink-and-drive case once, and I had to bail her out. They were returning from a party. While growing up, she used to be obedient and well-mannered, but he spoiled her.

She even started lying to us about her life. We started to drift apart after he arrived. Two years back, on Eid day, she invited him to our home and introduced him to us. We didn't take it well, and we had a huge fight. We tried to tell her how he was wrong for her, but finally, she left with him. I'm sure he's involved in her death, or at least he has something to do with it."

Marc reassured him, "If he's involved, we'll make sure he pays. Can you tell us about Tracey and Hina?"

Sajid explained, "The three of them were best friends and were inseparable. Hina is my brother's daughter; she was Maysa's cousin, and Tracey was her school friend. After school, Tracey became a dancer and performer, and Maysa went to university, so they started meeting less often. Tracey is a good dancer and performer and has recently performed for Cirque du Soleil."

Marc inquired, "Besides James, do you have doubts about anyone else? Was she having problems with anyone?"

Sajid replied, "Not that we know of. She was a well-to-do, self-sufficient girl. I don't think anyone could have any problem with her."

"Thank you for the information," Marc acknowledged. "One final question: where were you today in the evening, around 4 PM to 6 PM?"

Sajid grew agitated. "As I already told you, we were completely booked today, so I was at my restaurant, ensuring everything was prepared for our guests in the evening. Then I went home, picked up Najma and Roohi, and went to Maysa's place."

"I understand," Marc said. "If necessary, we will visit your restaurant. I'm sorry for your loss today. You are free to leave now. It's almost 10 at night, and it's getting late for Roohi. We will contact you again if needed. And please, if you plan to leave town, inform us beforehand."

Sajid and Najma left with Roohi, who was waiting with Antoine.

Chapter 3:
The Next day

Marc and Aynaz reviewed the notes Aynaz had taken during her previous conversation with Sajid and Najma.

Aynaz inquired, "I was wondering yesterday, why did you specifically ask them to bring Roohi to the police station even though you never planned to talk to her?"

Marc explained, "The psychological manipulation of interrogation should begin much before the interrogator even opens his mouth. Roohi's presence could have acted as a trigger point for them. Knowing that their only daughter was also in potential danger might have compelled them to confess or divulge crucial information about the crime. Additionally, I never intended to question a minor unless I had concrete evidence. From experience, I know such experiences can have a lasting impact on a child's psyche."

Aynaz probed further, "What did you conclude from that conversation? Do you think they were involved in the murder?"

Marc reflected, "Parents often create a protective bubble around their children, shielding them from the outside world. However, they sometimes overlook checking how their child is faring within that bubble. It's crucial for parents not only to shield their children from external threats but also to understand their inner thoughts, feelings, and emotions. If a child feels insecure or harbors negative thoughts without the parents noticing, it could lead to catastrophic outcomes."

"In this case, Sajid seemed to have idealized his daughter as innocent and lovely, unable to conceive of her engaging in a behavior he wouldn't approve of. This led to a state of bewilderment when confronted with her actions, such as introducing James. If Sajid had listened to and understood his daughter's perspective that day, the situation might have unfolded differently."

"My opinion on whether they did it depends on how orthodox Sajid's beliefs are and how much he cares about his social image. As he said, he is a very religious and respected man in the community, and very religious and reputed people tend to sometimes act in ways that are unimaginable and unspeakable in the name of God or reputation, lest they lose their standing. Now, all we need to know is if Maysa did something that could have triggered him to do this. We will see that in the future as we unfold this mystery further."

Aynaz took a deep breath and expressed, "It is strange that from the moment a child is born, they spend the most time with their parents, yet they feel afraid to reach out to them if anything troubles them. I only wish that parents could understand their children better and create a more nurturing environment. So, even if a child has a problem, they can easily reach out to their parents without hesitation."

Marc nodded. Antoine entered the room, sensing the tension, and remained quiet, waiting for someone to speak.

Aynaz then gestured towards the notebook and said, "We have a few more names now: Tracey, Hina, James, and Andre to investigate."

Marc added, "There is one more name on that list, Rehan. But they never talked about him. Maybe they didn't know about Rehan. We will question them after we get the medical reports."

Marc turned to Antoine, inquiring, "Was there any word from the restaurant owner who delivered that food to Maysa's house?"

Antoine responded, "Yes, they told me it was ordered by Maysa's account around 4:45 PM. I then questioned the delivery person who delivered that order. He said he reached the apartment at around 5:40 PM. He told me that he saw a man leaving the apartment just as he entered the corridor from the lift. That man was locking the apartment door, appeared to be in a hurry, and looked panicked. The delivery man then knocked on the door a couple of times, but no one answered, so he left the parcel outside the apartment and departed. Also, I confirmed that the delivery man's shoe size was eleven. At least one mystery is solved now."

Marc inquired, "Did he see that man's face or appearance?"

Antoine answered, "He said that he didn't get a very good look at the face, but he told me the man was not too tall, around 5 '9 feet, and looked physically fit. He was young and had a beard on his face. He believed the man was of South Asian origin, possibly from the Indian subcontinent."

Marc nodded thoughtfully. "I believe I have an idea who that might be. We should gather up all the people close to Maysa and ask him to identify if he could recognize anyone from them. We are certain of one thing at least that the killer was close to her."

He continued, "What about her phone? Did we find anything else from that? Anything from her social accounts?"

Antoine replied, "The call records from the day of the murder are consistent, and we found nothing suspicious. We are still trying to access her social media accounts to see if we find any relevant information there."

Marc inquired further, "Has the medical examination been completed, and the body released?"

Antoine responded, "The medical examination has been conducted, and samples have been taken for further testing. However, the official report will take approximately another week to generate. The body, however, will be released tonight."

"Good," Marc acknowledged. "Please keep me updated on any progress. Also, arrange a session with the delivery boy, and let's gather everyone to see if we can catch our killer."

Antoine noted, "I will arrange that. However, there is a funeral scheduled tomorrow at Sajid's home."

"Understood," Marc said. "Arrange the session for the day after. We have a funeral to attend tomorrow."

Chapter 4:
The Funeral

Scene 1: Burial

It was the third day of the murder, and preparations were made for her final rituals. It is a common saying or teaching in Islam not to delay the burial of the dead, and Sajid wanted the same, as it was already a day past her death.

A whole community attends a Muslim funeral; there are high chances of finding people at the funeral who don't know the dead person or his or her family personally. The ritual starts by cleaning the body completely. It must be cleansed at least three times and must be cleansed by the spouse or a relative of the same sex. For example, if a female dies, then this responsibility goes to her husband or any female relative of her, like her mother, daughter, or sister. In this case, Najma cleansed her daughter's body and covered her body with clothing.

Positioning Maysa's body to face the Kaaba in Mecca, the holiest site in Islam, they shrouded her with three white sheets. With meticulous care, the sheets were draped over her, symbolizing purity and dignity in death. Closing her eyes and placing cotton in her nostrils, they secured the shroud with ropes, signifying the finality of her earthly journey.

Overwhelmed by grief, Najma found solace in the support of her family. Hina and Roohi, Maysa's cousin and sister, respectively, stood by her side, offering assistance in performing the sacred rites. Observers whispered words of sympathy, acknowledging the profound sorrow of a parent burying their child, a sentiment echoed in the collective prayers for divine comfort.

Once the body is prepared and the family has said their farewells, they gather for the funeral prayer. The deceased is positioned in front of the congregation, known as the Jamaat, facing the Kaaba, the sacred center of Islam. Led by an Imam or Muslim preacher, the prayer is offered almost in the same way as a normal prayer; they pray five times a day but without bowing down or Sajda. Mourners wear plain white traditional clothing as a sign of mourning, refraining from colorful or fashionable attire.

Imam Syed Ibrahim, a respected figure in Sajid's community, leads the prayer for Maysa, followed by all male attendees. This prayer holds significant importance in Islam, as it is believed to aid the deceased in their journey to the afterlife by seeking forgiveness for their earthly deeds.

Following the prayer, the body is taken to the burial site, where a grave has been prepared. The grave is dug parallel to Mecca and is deep enough to accommodate the deceased. The body is placed on its right side, facing Mecca, and then lowered into the grave. Mourners present at the burial throw three handfuls of soil onto the body, symbolizing the return to the earth. The grave is then filled with soil until it is level.

Montreal's Muslim cemetery, located in Laval near Montreal, serves as the final resting place for Maysa, where she is laid to rest according to these sacred rituals.

Additionally, Islamic teachings advise against excessive mourning, encouraging acceptance of death as an inevitable part of life. Muslims believe in living modestly and cultivating empathy for others, exemplified through practices such as fasting during Ramadan to strengthen their connection with God and foster compassion for humanity.

Scene 2: Sajid's home

After the burial, they returned to Sajid's home to pay their condolences. James, Hina, and Tracey attended the service and were present at Sajid's grand home in Westmount. The house, well-decorated and expansive, showcased Sajid's wealth. Despite his affluent lifestyle, Sajid's appearance remained unassuming.

Marc and Aynaz arrived, offering their condolences to Sajid and Najma. "Today, we came to support you in your hard time, and remember, whoever did this, we will find them. We are sorry for your loss," Marc expressed sympathetically.

They positioned themselves near a pillar, observing the gathering. Marc recognized this as a prime opportunity to observe potential suspects, as all of Maysa's close relatives were present. He remained vigilant for any signs of guilt or deception.

Sajid harbored anger towards James, holding him responsible for Maysa's death. However, Najma restrained him, understanding the importance of maintaining composure in their community. Though Sajid's emotions were evident, he refrained from confrontation. Marc noticed James's discomfort in response to Sajid's visible anger.

All attendees wore white attire, including James, who donned a white Salwar Kameez gifted by Maysa. This evoked memories and emotions in James, adding complexity to the gathering.

Hina appeared comfortable, moving among the guests with ease as she assisted in serving light refreshments and engaging them with anecdotes about Maysa. Her familiarity with the rituals and attendees allowed her to navigate the gathering effortlessly. Sajid and Najma remained withdrawn, their grief palpable, leading guests to refrain from expecting their active participation.

Observing Hina and Tracey conversing, Marc approached them, introducing himself, "Hello, I'm Marc, the investigating officer for this case."

Tracey questioned, "How can you be certain this was a murder and not suicide or natural death?"

Marc explained, "No one in a sound state of mind would order food before taking their own life. Additionally, we haven't found any motive for suicide. Maysa was doing well both professionally and personally."

Though Tracey didn't press further, she seemed unconvinced by Marc's assurance regarding Maysa's personal life.

Turning to Hina, Marc acknowledged, "I understand you were Maysa's cousin and have known her for years. But were you close to her as well?"

Hina affirmed, "Yes, I was very close to her; she was not just my Cousin but also my best friend."

He then directed his attention to Tracey and asked, "How about you? How did you become friends and how close you were to her?".

Tracey hesitated before responding, "Is this interrogation? I'm sorry, but this doesn't seem like the right place for that."

Aynaz interjected reassuringly, "No, this isn't an interrogation. Feel free to answer or not, but your input could help us understand your friend better and potentially aid in solving this mystery."

Noticing Tracey's discomfort, Hina intervened, "I can answer this question, but only if Tracey agrees. It's been a long time, Tracey. It's okay not to shy away from it anymore."

With a gesture, Tracey indicated that Hina should continue.

Hina proceeded, "This story illustrates Maysa's maturity and empathy, as well as a poignant moment for Tracey. In fifth grade, Maysa and I were classmates and spent a lot of time together. We had a social engagement class where we were tasked with getting to know someone in the class better. One day, Maysa noticed Tracey sitting alone in the corner, not engaging with anyone. Despite Tracey's initial reluctance, Maysa approached her, attempting to strike up a conversation."

She then sat next to her silently. This routine repeated for weeks, with Maysa consistently sitting by Tracey's side. One day, I felt a pang of jealousy and asked Maysa why she kept trying to engage with Tracey when she showed no interest. Maysa explained that Tracey didn't have any friends because she didn't trust anyone enough to share her thoughts. Maysa believed that by being present for Tracey, she could gradually earn her trust and perhaps become her friend. That was Maysa's maturity, even at a young age."

As Hina reminisced about this memory, Tracey's eyes welled up with tears.

Hina continued, "Tracey had a troubled childhood. Up until the fifth grade, she refused to speak to anyone in class. Her hostile behavior often led to visits to the principal's office, and she once even bit a classmate who tried to engage with her. The school attempted to address her behavior by recommending therapy, but her parents, struggling financially and overwhelmed by multiple jobs, were unable to pursue it."

"Maysa persisted in approaching Tracey, simply sitting beside her without disturbing her. She aimed to break through Tracey's protective barrier, where no one else was allowed. Near the end of the term, Maysa sat beside Tracey in a social engagement class and encouraged her to speak, as it might be their last opportunity to interact before the class concluded."

Tracey turned her face towards her, tears streaming down her cheeks. Without a word, she wrapped her arms tightly around her, seeking solace in her embrace. The weight of Tracey's sorrow pressed against her, and she held her close, offering comfort in the silence of their shared grief. It was a moment of profound connection, one that spoke volumes in its simplicity. Witnessing the depth of compassion and maturity in such a young child left her spellbound, her heart heavy with emotion as she watched them embrace, tears mingling in their shared sorrow.

Hina then paused to take a deep breath and continued, "Then the teacher took both of them into another empty classroom where some more faculties joined them, and this time Tracey told them everything. She told them that she was getting abused by her uncle, who was also her neighbor. She said that it started almost two years ago when her parents went out of the station, and he was the one in charge of babysitting her. At that point in time, she couldn't understand much, but she felt scared after it happened. After that day, he often called her to his home and did horrific things to her. She was still going through that hell, but she didn't have the courage or the understanding to complain about him. If it hadn't been for Maysa's intervention, then God only knows how long that would have continued. She created a sense of trust by not giving up on Tracey, just sitting right next to her every time in that class, and by letting Tracey build the trust she had lost because of her vicious uncle. Once Tracey had built that trust for Maysa, it was like she had gained trust in humanity again, and this helped her gather the courage to speak up for herself and speak her heart out. Her uncle was found guilty and was given life imprisonment, and we three have never been separated since."

Hina fell silent, her gaze shifting to Tracey as she wrapped her in a comforting embrace. Marc and Aynaz stood nearby, their expressions reflecting sadness and concern.

With tearful eyes and a heart full of warmth, Tracey spoke softly, "Mers was the best, and I loved her dearly. I named her Mers from 'Merci' because I believed she was a divine gift, a mercy bestowed upon me. It also means 'thank you' in French, and I was eternally grateful for her presence."

Moved by Tracey's words, Marc expressed his condolences, "I am deeply sorry that you endured such pain as a child. I wish those who commit such heinous acts against children would face harsher consequences than mere imprisonment. However, hearing that Maysa had such caring and supportive friends is heartening."

*****

On the other side of the hall, James grew increasingly

suspicious of the prolonged conversation between Marc, Hina, and Tracey. His disdainful glare intensified each time he passed by Sajid, and his restlessness became palpable.

Observing Tracey standing alone, James seized the opportunity to pull her aside, whispering impatiently, "What were you talking to that detective about? I'm losing my mind here, and this Sajid is becoming unbearable. I just want to leave."

Meanwhile, Marc, noticing their hushed conversation, discreetly positioned himself behind a nearby pillar in an attempt to eavesdrop.

Tracey responded softly, "I understand, but we must endure a bit longer. If we act suspiciously, people might start to suspect us, especially considering the circumstances surrounding the murder."

Though Marc struggled to hear their conversation clearly due to their proximity and subdued voices, he couldn't shake off the suspicion arising from James and Tracey's apparent comfort.

James then noticed a shadow cast on the floor, prompting him to gesture towards Tracey. Afterward, they entered the hall and joined Hina, engaging in casual conversation.

Meanwhile, Marc approached Aynaz, expressing his suspicion about Tracey and James. He instructed her to keep an eye on them while he wandered the hall, eavesdropping on conversations in hopes of uncovering any clues. Amidst the chatter, Marc overheard rumors implicating Sajid and James in Maysa's murder. Dismissing these rumors as baseless gossip fueled by hatred, Marc continued his investigation.

Later, Marc approached Aynaz and inquired about Rehan's

presence at the gathering. Aynaz confirmed that Rehan was not in attendance, as verified by Hina.

Marc made a mental note of the rumors circulating about Sajid's potential involvement in Maysa's murder and pondered whether Sajid could genuinely be capable of such a heinous act to preserve his reputation in the community. The insinuations about Sajid's motives added another layer of complexity to the investigation, prompting Marc to delve deeper into Sajid's personal and social life dynamics.

As Marc contemplated the implications of the rumors, he approached James with a sense of camaraderie, acknowledging that James likely knew of his role as the detective tasked with solving the murder mystery. This interaction hinted at the investigation's underlying tension and secrecy, setting the stage for further developments in the narrative.

James replied, "Yes, indeed she mentioned you sometime back and Hina as well. How are you doing, detective? And thank you for attending the funeral."

Marc nodded, a somber expression on his face. "I wouldn't have missed it at any cost. I have heard you are an actor and a good one."

"Thank you," James said with a modest smile. "You must come sometime to watch me. I perform in the auditorium at Place-Des-Arts."

Marc agreed with a polite nod, and then James excused himself, maintaining the decorum of the occasion. Despite the formalities, Marc couldn't shake the feeling of needing to delve deeper, to look into James's eyes and question him.

Scene 3: Andre's Entry

Sajid was engaged with guests when a striking young man entered the hall and made his way directly to him. Tall, well-built, with dark skin, he offered his condolences in French before seamlessly switching to English with a French accent.

"Je suis désolé," he began. "I am so sorry for your loss. Maysa was a wonderful woman, very talented at her job."

Sajid acknowledged his presence with gratitude. "Thank you for coming, Andre. Yes, she was truly wonderful, and that's why so many have gathered today to remember her."

Andre expressed his regret at the dreams they shared for their company, which were now disrupted by Maysa's untimely departure. Aynaz, overhearing the conversation, felt a sense of skepticism at Andre's words, sensing an insincerity beneath his polished exterior. However, she couldn't deny his physical appeal, noting his striking appearance in a simple white shirt and trousers.

Andre then approached James, whom he knew from accompanying Maysa on her office trips.

"I am so sorry about your loss," Andre offered sincerely, extending his condolences.

James, however, saw through Andre's facade and dismissed his condolences with a blunt retort. "I know you don't mean a word, so just save it for later," he said before walking away, leaving Andre standing alone.

Marc observed the tense exchange of emotions but chose not to delve deeper into the matter at that moment.

However, Sajid, fueled by his fury towards James and his perception of disrespect towards their guest, could not restrain himself. He stormed over to James, his anger palpable as he criticized him for his alleged role in Maysa's death. Sajid's accusations hung heavily in the air, leaving James shocked and speechless.

Ignoring James's silence, Sajid continued his verbal assault, expressing his profound grief and placing the blame squarely on James's shoulders. Despite James's emotional reaction, he remained silent, his eyes fixed on the ground.

The tense confrontation was interrupted by Tracey, who swiftly intervened, urging Sajid to reconsider his accusations and asserting James's innocence. Najma, sensing the escalating tension, intervened as well, leading Sajid away from the confrontation.

Meanwhile, Tracey stood by James's side, offering him support and solidarity before eventually escorting him away from the scene.

Marc observed the dynamics between James, Tracey, and Sajid, noting the complex interplay of emotions and hatred.

Following the confrontation, Sajid announced the conclusion of the ceremony, signaling everyone to depart.

Chapter 5:
The delivery boy

It had been two days since the funeral, Marc and Antoine were still trying to find Rehan, who was the only close friend who missed the funeral and had been missing since the day of the murder. His cell phone was unreachable, and he'd vanished from sight for nearly a week. This alarming disappearance prompted Marc to launch a search. Armed with a search warrant, they combed his home but found no answers. Contacting Rehan's parents in India yielded no information about his whereabouts, although it did induce panic in his household. Marc hoped this would pressure Rehan into revealing himself or making mistakes that would lead to his capture. Confirming with airlines, they found no evidence of Rehan flying to India. Marc even attempted to contact the Delhi police to search Rehan's parents' house, suspecting they might be hiding him.

Increasingly convinced of Rehan's involvement in Maysa's murder, Marc understood that mere speculation wouldn't secure his punishment; he needed concrete evidence.

For a real detective, it is not enough to find out who committed the crime; it is also important to find out why they did it and what the motivation behind it was. Was it greed, lust, love, envy, fear, or any other of the major sins? Marc also wanted to know this and was trying his best to find him to quench his thirst for curiosity.

At around 4:00 pm, Antoine entered Marc's office, where Marc was writing down some notes for another case he was handling.

Antoine announces with shortness in his breadth, "We have found Rehan. He was hiding in his sister's place in California, and one of our officers is right now escorting him to the police station. They should be here in an hour or so."

Marc stood up from his chair with excitement and said, "That's good news now; we don't need to ask for help from the Indian police."

"Can you please arrange with the delivery boy to identify the person he saw on the murder day when Rehan is here and also call James and Sajid for identification?"

At around 7:15 pm, Rehan entered the station with his hands cuffed and his head held low. Rehan was in his late twenties. He was good-looking, well built, not too tall or short, around 5'9 feet with brown skin but with untidy stubble. He was wearing a white t-shirt tight on his shoulders and biceps, blue denim jeans, and white sneakers. He looked like he could easily get lucky in a bar or a pub on a good day.

James, Sajid, and the delivery boy were already present at the station, but all were waiting in different cabins, as Marc didn't want anyone to influence the identification process.

There is a law that if a witness sees the suspect in a handcuff before identifying the accused, then his statement becomes inadmissible in court as it will be seen as hindering the witness.

He instructed Antoine to escort Rehan directly to the identification room and remove his handcuffs. Aynaz was tasked with bringing Sajid and James to the same room, positioning them one hand's distance apart and facing the mirror.

The identification room featured a large mirror adorning one of its walls, serving as a two-way glass for observation. All three individuals were positioned and ready, standing in anticipation.

Meanwhile, Marc escorted the delivery boy to an adjacent room, ensuring he remained out of sight of the others while maintaining a clear view of them. This precaution was taken for witness protection and to facilitate unbiased identification. Despite Marc's conviction that Rehan was the culprit, he sought concrete evidence for presentation in court, though his confidence in Rehan's guilt remained unwavering.

Tension simmered between Rehan and James inside the room, their exchanged glances laden with hostility. Despite the restrained environment of the police station, the palpable animosity hinted at a potential confrontation brewing beneath the surface. Meanwhile, Sajid's weariness was evident as he found himself once again summoned to the station, yet he knew he couldn't refuse, given the gravity of his daughter's situation.

The delivery boy entered and faced the glass. It was James first, and momentarily he said, "The man I saw was of a darker tone."

Then he took a step further down the room, stood in front of Sajid, and started staring at him. After staring at him and observing him for a few minutes, he said, "This could be the man I saw that day. He was brown as he was and of the same height. Since he was wearing a long coat and a hat that day, I could not properly notice his face, but he could be him."

Marc, taken aback by this revelation, sought clarification on the certainty of his identification. He conceded that he wasn't entirely sure but acknowledged that Sajid bore enough resemblance to the suspect to warrant consideration.

A whirlwind of thoughts raced through Marc's mind as he urged the witness to identify the last man. Taking a step closer to Rehan, Marc scrutinized him before turning to the witness for confirmation.

After a long time of observing him, he turned to Marc and said, "This could also be that man I saw that day. I could be wrong also, but I think I saw someone like him that day."

Aware that this identification alone would not suffice to incriminate Rehan but could be sufficient to take him into custody. He pondered over his next moves and realized that securing a confession would be crucial to solidifying Rehan's guilt. Ordering Antoine to record the witness's statements, Marc instructed him to release the witness and take Rehan into custody for further questioning.

Chapter 6:
Rehan's Interrogation

Scene 1: Turmoil

Rehan sat inside the lock-up of the downtown Montreal police station, his mind consumed by the events leading up to his arrest. More than 24 hours had passed since he was taken into custody. Initially, he had protested vehemently, asserting his innocence with tears and shouts. But now, exhaustion settled over him, enveloping his thoughts in a blanket of calmness.

In this moment of despair, Rehan found himself reflecting on crucial moments of his life. He remembered the joy and pride in his parents' eyes when he graduated from college with a degree in computer science. Their happiness swelled when he secured a job offer from a prestigious software company in Canada. Recalling the tearful goodbye at the airport, with his mother's sobs echoing in his ears, Rehan felt a pang of heartbreak. Despite the emotional turmoil, he knew he had to leave for the promise of a better life and future opportunities.

Memories of his college friends' envy and congratulations flooded his mind. They had admired his chance to build a luxurious life abroad. Yet, amidst the excitement, Rehan couldn't shake the feeling of being torn away from his loved ones, embarking on a journey fraught with uncertainty.

His heart weighed heavy with remorse as he reflected on the sacrifices he had made, leaving behind his homeland to start anew in a foreign country. The fear gnawed at him, imagining the disappointment his parents would feel, branding him a criminal. The thought of his friends' pity and the potential ostracization from his community filled him with dread. The looming prospect of a tarnished reputation and the inability to forgive himself tormented him relentlessly.

He questioned what misstep led him to this lonely cell, confined behind bars. The gravity of his predicament was not lost to him; a guilty verdict or even the mere accusation would obliterate his career prospects, rendering him untouchable in the job market with a criminal record. His troubled mind welled with tears; his anguish palpable.

Amidst the turmoil, his thoughts drifted to his life in Canada and memories of Maysa. Arriving five years prior, he thrived professionally, securing two promotions, and anticipated further success in the coming year. Their encounter at a company conference sparked a connection, with Maysa seeking to engage his company as a client for her successful startup venture.

Maysa, a software engineer and CEO of an artificial intelligence company in Montreal specializes in data gathering from customer service calls. Their innovative approach involved converting speech to text and then analyzing the data to glean market insights and customer feedback. Maysa's professionalism and expertise in the field made her instrumental in the company's success.

Upon meeting Maysa, Rehan felt an instant connection drawn to her shared cultural background and professional interests. Their frequent meetings for work discussions soon evolved into a close friendship. However, when Maysa confided in him about her relationship with James, Rehan's feelings took a complicated turn. He harbored affection for Maysa but resigned himself to the fact that a sincere relationship with her was not possible.

Despite this realization, he continued to flirt with Maysa and express his feelings through sweet messages, relishing the newfound confidence and excitement that came with their interactions. Maysa, perceived as a forbidden fruit, became a source of fascination for Rehan, driving him to pursue her despite the inherent risks.

As Rehan reflects on his feelings from within his lonely cell, he grapples with the consequences of his actions, realizing that his pursuit of Maysa has led to unforeseen challenges and heartache.

Scene 2: Interrogation

Antoine entered the cell and instructed Rehan to prepare himself for interrogation. Rehan immediately demanded legal representation before proceeding.

"Today is Saturday night, Rehan. You will have to wait until Monday to see a lawyer," Antoine retorted, compelling Rehan to stand up and push him out of the cell.

Rehan persisted, "You can't do this to me. Without legal counsel, I will not make any statements. Why didn't you question me yesterday when I could arrange for a lawyer? You have kept me locked up for 24 hours without proper evidence. I will report this misconduct in court."

Antoine smirked in response, "Yeah, we'll see about that."

Rehan felt a wave of terror, knowing that his disappearance on the night of the murder would inevitably cast suspicion upon him.

As he entered the interrogation room, he found Marc already seated on one side of the table, with Aynaz positioned in a corner, affording her a clear view of the room. On one wall, a large mirror provided visibility from the adjoining room, from which Rehan could be seen clearly. The room's centerpiece was a brown table surrounded by four chairs, two on each side. Observing a camera with a blinking red light in the top right corner, Rehan could not shake the feeling that the surveillance extended beyond what was immediately apparent.

This was Rehan's first time inside one of these interrogation rooms, and he found himself overwhelmed with emotions. Antoine guided him to a seat opposite Marc before exiting the room.

Observing Rehan's nervous state, Marc attempted to reassure him. "You don't need to be afraid. We will only ask some basic questions."

Despite Marc's attempt to calm him, Rehan remained visibly frightened, shaking with fear.

In an effort to further soothe Rehan's nerves, Marc continued, "You were shouting that you are innocent and have nothing to do with the murder. If that is true, let us know what happened so we can help you."

Meeting Marc's gaze, Rehan took a deep breath, gradually calming himself down.

Marc proceeded with his questioning. "I know you are here on a work permit and by profession you are a software engineer. But what I am interested to know about is how did you two meet?"

He took a second before speaking and said, "We met at a conference in my company. She was there to attend it and pitch about her company to get my company as her client."

Marc pressed further, insinuating, "So, she was there for work, and you started hitting on her."

Reacting defensively, Rehan shouted, "No! I am not like that. I never had any relationship. I was a nerd in college, and we were just friends."

Marc handed him a piece of paper, pointing out, "So you are saying you send these text messages to every woman you know?"

Feeling a twinge of embarrassment, Rehan admitted, "Yes, I sent her these text messages, but we were not in love, and we were not in a relationship. She was in a relationship with James, and we were just friends."

Marc acknowledged, "Yes, you said that already."

Aynaz interrupted, her voice cutting through the tension in the room. "How I see this is plain and simple. You were in love with her, but she didn't reciprocate your love and rejected you because she loved James. After trying for one year, you gave up on her and decided to kill her as you were not able to see her with anyone else."

Marc nodded, considering her words. "Yes, that completely makes sense, and it is a strong motive for the murder."

Rehan's reaction was immediate and intense. He jumped out of his chair furiously and shouted, "I never murdered her! These are false accusations. I am innocent!"

Marc stood from his chair, his demeanor firm. "Then what were you doing at her apartment on the day of the murder, and why were you in hiding? An innocent man would never do so."

Rehan's tears were evident as he looked down at the desk, his voice trembling with emotion. "I was hiding because I was afraid that everyone would think it was me. Yes, I went to her apartment that day. I was supposed to pick her up, and we were going to see Tracey's performance that night. I reached her apartment and knocked at her door for some time, but she didn't open the door. So, I used the spare key that she kept under her doormat to get inside the apartment, which I normally do in case she is not at home, and I have to wait for her. Upon entering, I was shocked to see her lying unconscious on the table. I ran to her and checked her pulse in case I needed to call the hospital, but she wasn't breathing. I was terrified and couldn't understand what to do. I just didn't want any trouble, as I am on a work permit here, and if I were caught, even if I wasn't jailed, I would have been deported back, jobless. There was so much at stake for me that my whole career would have been jeopardized. I couldn't think clearly at the moment, so I just left her lying dead and fled from the site. While closing the door behind me, the delivery boy saw me, but I still ran off. I knew he would recognize me, so I ran off to my sister's place. I am ashamed of what I did, but I did not kill her. She was already dead when I reached there. I just panicked and didn't understand what to do."

After a brief pause, he continued to defend himself, questioning why he would have any motive to harm the victim. He emphasized their close friendship, highlighting how they bonded over shared experiences and cultural backgrounds. He explained that their relationship was purely platonic, rooted in mutual understanding and support during challenging times. He even disclosed personal details about his own arranged marriage, indicating a level of trust and openness between them. However, he adamantly denied any romantic involvement, asserting that he was merely in the wrong place at the wrong time.

He further said, "I was filling a void in her life by being a friend that understands her."

Marc pressed further, questioning the dynamics of the victim's friendships and support network, and asked, "What do you mean her other friends wouldn't understand her? Hina is also Indian, and I am sure she would have listened to her."

He replied, "What all looks that simple is not that simple. Hina was also not 100% supportive of her relationship with James."

Meanwhile, Aynaz diligently observed the suspect's demeanor and choice of words, jotting down notes in her notepad, capturing subtle cues that might provide valuable insights into his testimony.

After two minutes of tense silence, Marc broke it with a calculated response, his tone laced with accusation. "I don't buy a word you just said. You know what I think? I think you were after her for her money and status in Canada, which would have helped you to stay here without fear. After all, she was doing well and was from a reputable family. When you realize that her parents are against her relationship, you think you will be there for her, and she will eventually agree to marry you. That's why you always flirted with her. But when you saw she was still not giving up on James, you planned to murder her. That is what you did in response to it."

Aynaz discerned Marc's tactic, attempting to provoke a

response that could aid their investigation. She countered, "Yes, otherwise why would you still flirt with her knowing she already has a boyfriend?"

Rehan, feeling defensive, retorted, "Why am I the only one who is wrong here? Why is the boy always wrong in these situations? Was the girl not involved? Was I forcing myself on her? No sir, she liked it too. She liked the attention. Not once did she ever say to me to stop or not to talk to her like that. She was enjoying the attention I was giving her, which James was not giving her. On the contrary, we talked for hours; sometimes we talked the whole night. Now, will you consider her also wrong here, or what was her motivation for doing so? For your information, I had never planned to stay here long, but I have plans to move back anyway and get married back in India. Now, where does your hypothesis stand here? I also have chats and proof of my plans."

Marc then, with a visible grin on his face asked, "What do you mean by James not giving her enough attention?"

Rehan processed the weight of his own words, realizing he had potentially walked into a trap. He spoke cautiously, revealing a glimpse into James and Maysa's tumultuous relationship.

"James had an accident about one and a half years ago. It left him with severe facial injuries, which, for an actor, were doubly devastating. Directors began to drop him from plays, citing the need for rest and recovery. Financially and emotionally drained, James's confidence plummeted, and their relationship suffered as a result. Sajid, Maysa's father, was also unsupportive during this challenging time."

As Rehan spoke, the complexity of Maysa's situation became apparent. He continued, shedding light on his role in her life.

"I entered her life during this tumultuous period. Initially, I harbored romantic feelings, but as I grew to understand her struggles, I realized she couldn't handle another emotional burden. Instead, we developed a close friendship. Whenever she needed someone to confide in, she turned to me. I would lift her spirits with playful banter and companionship, providing a brief respite from her troubles."

Marc then probed for further details, seeking to understand Maysa's hardships more deeply.

"What specific challenges did she face during this time? Can you provide any examples?"

He replied, "Problems with James; his behavior toward her was inappropriate. He was broke so he couldn't take her out anymore. And if sometimes she took him out, he would behave very badly with her as he considered that as a charity towards him. He even mistreated her in front of others in a restaurant. She once told me that she took him out to one of the terrace restaurants to celebrate her new client, but he became so jealous that he shouted at her and left her alone in that restaurant crying. Jealousy and insecurity had taken over him, and we all know that if these things come into a relationship, then it becomes a sinking ship. She was still trying to make it afloat and was trying to do whatever she could to make him feel happy and make things work between them."

After a short pause, he continued, "This reached the level that he started doubting her fidelity towards the relationship. He started following her sometimes to the office or other places to see if she was indeed going where she said she was or to whom she was meeting. He checked her phone regularly and did some other awful things that she didn't even tell me. He started picking her up from work so that she wouldn't go anywhere else. He had put all his energy into these negative things instead of improving himself."

Marc said, "I didn't notice any scars on James' face."

He replied, "Yes, he has done surgery to get them removed, which she has paid for. I am not sure if he did this or not, but I wouldn't be surprised to know that he did it."

Marc then looked at Aynaz and asked her to take him back to his cell.

*****

After returning Rehan to his cell, Aynaz entered Marc's office, seeking his opinion on the recent interrogation.

"Marc, what are your thoughts?" she inquired.

"I'm not entirely convinced by Rehan's testimony. But what he said is possible, so we should consider James a prime suspect as well."

Aynaz nodded, acknowledging Marc's observation. "Yes, his demeanor seemed sincere, and he remained steadfast despite your attempts to provoke him. Either he's exceptionally good at deception, or he's telling the truth."

Marc fell into a thoughtful silence before expressing his sentiments. "If Rehan's account is accurate, then I would be deeply disappointed in James, not just for the murder itself, but also for how he treated her. Relationships can't be coerced. Love must be freely given and reciprocated. Forcing someone to love you is futile and only leads to inevitable turmoil."

"Indeed," Aynaz agreed. "Understanding this principle could resolve countless conflicts. However, partial knowledge often exacerbates problems. We must seek to understand all perspectives."

Marc nodded in agreement. "Yes, we should speak to one more person."

Concerning Rehan's status, Aynaz inquired, "What about Rehan? Should we release him?"

Marc deliberated before responding, "Keep him detained for now. If the murderer is still at large, keeping Rehan in custody may prompt them to make a mistake, believing they have evaded capture. Also, could you arrange for Antoine to bring James to the station tomorrow for further questioning?"

With that, Aynaz left Marc's office, leaving him lost in contemplation.

Chapter 7:
James Interrogation

Marc strolled into his office, his mind consumed with the lingering mystery of the unsolved murder. "It has been seven days since the murder, and we are in no way near the murderer," he murmured to himself, frustration evident in his tone. Reflecting on the suspects, he pondered Rehan's potential involvement, considering his motive for revenge. However, doubts arose after hearing Rehan's testimony, casting uncertainty on his guilt. "Was he telling the truth about James?" Marc questioned, contemplating the credibility of each suspect. The elusive nature of the truth left him feeling uncertain and overwhelmed. "Je ne sais pas!"

Interrupting his thoughts, Aynaz entered the office with news of James's presence in the interrogation room. "We have James waiting for you in the interrogation room," she announced, prompting Marc to refocus his attention on the task at hand.

Entering the interrogation room, Marc observed James's composed demeanor, a stark contrast to his behavior at the funeral. The shift in James's demeanor left Marc considering the possibility of innocence or calculated deception. Despite lacking concrete evidence, Marc remained vigilant and aware of the investigation's intricacies.

Seating himself opposite James, Marc noted subtle changes in

James's appearance, hinting at a potential disguise. Maintaining a friendly demeanor, Marc greeted James in French, "Ça va, James?" concealing his suspicions behind a facade of civility.

James smiled back and said, "Ça va bien, et vous Marc?"

Marc replied, "I am good too, Merci. I have called you here to learn more about you and Maysa. Things are pointing out that your relationship was going through a rough patch. Is it true?"

"What? Rough patch? No way, rather, we were closer to each other than we ever were. I went through a tough time personally, but that helped us grow closer to each other. She helped me to survive that," as he replied, his voice tinged with emotion.

Marc nodded, acknowledging James's response. "Okay, let's start from the beginning then. How did you two meet?"

James rolled his eyes up without lifting his face and reflected for a moment before replying, "It was five years ago, but I still remember each second of that day. It was the last day of my play. Tracey was also a part of the play as a dancer. The play was a tremendous success; it ran for almost four months, and all the shows were almost completely booked. It was the closing night, and as usual, we celebrated the closing night of a successful play. Tracey had also invited Maysa to the party. Although I was intoxicated, I still remember her and how she looked that day. She was wearing a pair of blue ripped jeans, high white heels, and a loose white shirt with a plain white t-shirt under it. I don't know if it was because of the alcohol, but her eyes were glittering that night. The place was packed with people, yet I was able to notice it from anywhere in the room that night. She was the face-turner at that party, and the moment I laid my eyes on her, I was mesmerized. Luckily, she was with Tracey, and Tracey and I had become good friends during that play. I walked over to Tracey, and she introduced us. The music was loud, so not many words were exchanged, but I hung out with them for the rest of the evening, dancing to the music together."

Continuing with a slightly softer tone, he began, "I took her number that day, and we started messaging each other. We talked till late at night, sharing our thoughts, ambitions, goals, fears, and everything in between. We started meeting often after that, and she sooner than I realized, she became a constant presence in my life. Maysa attended almost all my plays, supporting me in ways I never expected. We delved into deep conversations, exploring topics ranging from our daily routines to our dreams for the future. Despite coming from vastly different backgrounds, we found common ground and endless topics to discuss."

Pausing for a moment, he collected his thoughts before adding, "During that time, Maysa was facing significant pressure and stress at work. She had just graduated and was starting her own company, but her parents were pressuring her to marry. Despite her maturity and education, they believed marriage should be her ultimate goal. This conflict weighed heavily on her, causing her considerable distress."

"It's important to understand that while Maysa was Muslim and Indian, she was also a product of a Canadian upbringing. She embraced diversity and had a wide circle of friends from various backgrounds. Her desire to achieve more in life clashed with her parents' traditional expectations, sometimes leaving her feeling suffocated. Our conversations provided her with an outlet to release her pent-up stress and share her aspirations and challenges. What I admired most about Maysa was her ambition and determination to make a meaningful impact in the world. How often do you encounter a partner who not only motivates you but also helps you grow into a better person?"

Marc observed James speaking passionately about Maysa and pondered whether it stemmed from genuine love or perhaps veered into obsession. James's sentiments contradicted what Rehan had previously disclosed. As Marc navigated through the conflicting accounts, he sought to uncover the truth.

Acknowledging Maysa's admirable qualities, Marc extended his condolences before delving into a more personal inquiry. He broached the topic of James's past accident, prompting James to recount the harrowing experience. James detailed the trauma of the accident, its impact on his physical appearance as an actor, and the pivotal role Maysa played in his recovery. Despite facing professional setbacks, Maysa's unwavering support enabled James to navigate through his darkest moments and eventually resume his career.

With a subtle shift in conversation, Marc directed his attention to the matter at hand: James's knowledge of Rehan and his relationship with Maysa, "At what point in time did you come to know about Rehan, and how did you feel about their friendship?"

Marc saw how blood rushed down his face and made him red as his facial expression changed. He smirked in his head, thinking no matter how good of an actor you are, you can't hide hatred for someone.

He replied, "Well, he was not a friend, at least not a real friend of hers. He was just pretending to be a friend. He wanted to just be physical with her and then leave her. Even though he knew that she was committed, he kept flirting with her every day. He used to call her late at night and message her at odd times.

"I had to keep an eye on her phone just to make sure he was not seducing her to do something that would hurt her and also me. I had to start dropping her off at the office and picking her up whenever I could just to make sure he didn't follow her or force himself on her. Do you call that friendship?"

Marc replied, "Has she also felt the same way you did with him?"

James responded, "No, she was too sweet and innocent to think of him in this way. She never reciprocated his advances. I knew his main intentions, so I was trying to protect her from him."

Marc further inquired, "So, you are saying that Rehan was just trying to sleep with her, and they were not friends?"

James clarified, "She did consider him as a friend, but he didn't just see her as a friend; he wanted to get physical with her and leave her."

Marc probed further, "How can you be so sure about that?"

"Wasn't it obvious?" James grasped and continued, "The way he looked at her and talked to her. He used to ask her on dates knowing she was unavailable and used to text her cheesy messages all the time."

Marc countered, "But she never stopped him or asked him not to do all those things. Do you think maybe she liked him or talking to him, or maybe she liked the extra attention to herself and perhaps enjoying that?"

James replied, "I don't think so. I think she was just being polite to him as they had a lot of things in common and never stopped him. But he took that the wrong way and continued doing all those things."

Marc provokingly asked, "Maybe she was feeling a void in emotions from your end, and he filled that void for you? Why would a happy person go elsewhere looking for affection?"

This hit him hard, and he fell silent. Perhaps this was something he had been avoiding confronting for some time, choosing instead to blame Rehan for his lack of effort in the relationship and her pursuit of new friendships.

Lowering his gaze to the desk, he replied, "That could be one of the possible explanations, but that still doesn't mean he wasn't pursuing her just for physical intimacy. He didn't care much for her; otherwise, he would have attended the funeral, but he didn't."

Marc pondered over this. It was a valid argument—Rehan's absence from the funeral suggested a lack of genuine concern for Maysa. However, it didn't necessarily implicate him in her murder.

Marc asked, "Apart from Rehan, do you think anyone else had an issue with her or any other rivalry?"

James replied, "Do you know about Andre? He was present at her funeral."

Marc nodded, "Yes, I met him at the funeral. What about him?"

He replied, "I am not one hundred percent sure, but he and Maysa were not on excellent terms recently. As you might already know, they co-owned the company, but something you might not know is that their revenue depends on the new clients they bring to the company. Initially, they had this agreement that no matter who brought the client, it would be held under the company, and all the profits after expenses and employee payments would be divided equally between them. But when she realized that she was bringing in most of the clients and he was not making the same effort to acquire new clients, she insisted on the condition that profits would be based on the clients they brought to the company. This meant that the more clients or more prominent clients you bring to the company, the greater the profit percentage you would receive. So, they became somewhat competitive in acquiring clients, which initially benefited the company as both were actively pursuing new clients."

He further continued, "The problem arose when they both pursued the same client. She had been vying for a contract with a company for their new data analysis services. Unbeknownst to her, Rehan worked for the same company, and they crossed paths during her pitch. The potential contract could have significantly boosted her company's growth. Despite his efforts, Andre failed to secure the contract, leading to accusations from him. Around six months ago, they engaged in a heated argument, prompting thoughts to split the company. However, she managed to secure most of the clients, and that would have left him at a loss."

Marc contemplated the motive behind her death. With her passing, all the clients would now fall under Andre's sole ownership, eliminating any potential for a split. It seemed that he stood to gain substantially from her demise. Although Marc found this motive compelling, he remained cautious, acknowledging the possibility of ulterior motives and the role of money in such cases.

As their conversation drew to a close, Marc thanked him for his cooperation and reminded him, "Thank you for your time here and for helping us out. Do not leave the town without informing us, and we might ask you to be present again if needed. You may go now."

Marc and Aynaz convened in his office following the conversation.

Aynaz inquired, "What do you think? Was he telling the truth about Andre?"

Marc deliberated, "If it's true, then that gives him a strong motive for the murder. However, I'm not entirely convinced of this theory for some reason."

She opined that he could be responsible, perhaps not solely for financial gain but also to protect his reputation. As the co-owner of the company, he may have felt threatened by Maysa's dominant position. We both know how some men react when they feel overshadowed by a woman. They struggle to accept that women can excel in various fields, including networking and forging strong connections."

Marc nodded, acknowledging her perspective. "Yes, certain men have difficulty accepting being surpassed by a woman. We need to ascertain whether Andre falls into that category."

He then suggested, "Could you arrange a meeting with Andre tomorrow in his office?"

Aynaz assented with a nod before leaving the room to make the necessary arrangements.

Chapter 8:
Andre's office visit

Scene 1: Marc's Office

Aynaz entered Marc's office while he was engrossed in his daily newspaper, a visible sign of his growing impatience with the unsolved murder case. It had been nine days since the murder and five days since Rehan's arrest. Each lead seemed promising at first, only to lead to dead ends, leaving Marc frustrated and eager for a breakthrough.

"Good morning!" Aynaz announced, breaking the silence.

Marc glanced up from his newspaper, his expression reflecting a mix of weariness and anticipation. "Do you know, Aynaz, more than 70% of homicide cases in Canada are solved within the first 7 days of the murder?"

Aynaz gasped, understanding the gravity of the situation. "I have gathered the information on Andre as you requested."

Marc leaned forward; his interest piqued. "So, what did you find?"

Aynaz proceeded to share her findings. "I found out that money is not a concern for Andre. He comes from a very wealthy family, the Baudelaires."

Marc nodded, recognizing the significance of the name. "You mean The Baudelaires, the owners of the famous shoe-making company in Montreal."

"Yes," Aynaz confirmed. "They established the shoe business in the 1970s in Montreal and Quebec, eventually expanding across North America and into three continents. They are one of the biggest players in the shoe industry, with numerous showrooms worldwide."

Marc reflected on the Baudelaires' legacy. "His family has contributed significantly to the city. They've created jobs, invested in city projects and infrastructure, and have strong ties in politics. Given their reputation and influence, it will be a formidable task to implicate his son."

She replied, "He is not the son of Adam, the founding member of the company, but his younger brother Timmy. Timmy doesn't have strong control over the business, but he still holds a significant percentage of shares in the company, so they are also wealthy."

He asked rhetorically, "Then why did he start his own company and not get involved in his family business?"

She nodded and said, "He has lived in Montreal for the majority of his life and graduated from McGill University, where he met Maysa. They were on the same course. I also checked his social media accounts and found pictures of them together, especially old ones and some from college. He has been in a relationship with a girl named Claire for around two years now."

He asked, "Did you look into Claire? Who is she? Maybe

money was not the motive, but it could be something else since they knew each other for a long time and might have feelings for each other or may have had a fling before."

She replied, "No, I haven't looked into her. I figured she wasn't relevant for this case. Also, James told us that they were in constant competition and didn't like each other."

He responded, "More often than not, we overlook the faults in the people we love the most. Maybe James overlooked their relationship. Without a little spark, there is no fire."

She continued, "Regarding that fire, I inquired about them in his office and found out that they had a big fight not too long ago over their quarterly earnings result. Andre was heard cursing her and was upset with her. By the way, my informative response was that they were not too surprised by their fight, so I believe it had happened before as well."

He pondered, "So, James was right about the fights then, and there is more here than it seems. We need to look deeper into this situation. Where can I find him now?"

She replied, "Right now, he will be in his office on Wellington Street."

"Let's pay him a visit," he decided, picking up his coat as it was raining outside.

Scene 2: Andre's Office

Marc and Aynaz arrived at Andre's company on Wellington

Street, finding his office situated on the vibrant third floor of a four-story building. The workspace was bustling with activity, with around 50 employees working in the area. Desks were arranged side by side, and there were designated areas for employees to hang out, along with a nearby cafeteria for coffee and light snacks. Andre's office, located at the end of the floor, boasted a picturesque waterfront view from its window.

Approaching the receptionist for access to Andre's office, they were initially denied entry without a prior appointment. However, Marc's authoritative tone swiftly persuaded her to allow them access, emphasizing their role in investigating the murder of her late second boss. Sensing the urgency, she promptly informed Andre of their arrival.

Noticing Maysa's empty office adjacent to Andre's, Marc and Aynaz proceeded to enter Andre's office. The space exudes professionalism, with white walls and a glass wall offering a scenic view of the St. Lawrence River and the Vieux Port de Montreal. Andre greeted them and gestured for them to take a seat, indicating a table and chair on one end of the room and a two-seater sofa and coffee table on the other.

Anticipating their inquiry, Andre inquired, "So, how can I help you?"

Marc, straightforward as ever, replied, "You already know why we are here."

Andre acknowledged their purpose, speculating that they were there due to rumors about a dispute over earnings in the office.

Marc didn't confirm or deny but kept his gaze fixed on him.

He continued, "Well, having a fight over quarterly results

among company owners is not a big deal, especially in young companies like this. We have a very limited budget to invest in the company's expenditure and growth, which is included in the earnings report. So, if the expenditure exceeds the earnings, we won't have a net profit. Poor earnings reports reflect badly on our position in the market, resulting in fewer clients. This, in turn, leads to a decline in earnings, perpetuating a cycle that can ultimately lead to bankruptcy unless someone intervenes. In our case, we argued over the use of company funds for expenditure. At the beginning of each quarter or after reviewing our last quarter's profits, we would jointly decide on the amount of money we could allocate for the company's growth. This includes acquiring new clients, hiring staff, and expanding the company."

Marc asked, "Is acquiring a new client costly?"

He replied, "Absolutely, it is one of the costliest aspects. It involves expenses for travel, meetings, dinners, gifts, and even promotional offers for new clients. It's a considerable investment, and pursuing new clients can be challenging. However, in the last quarter, she exceeded the agreed-upon limit by almost double, with most of the expenditure allocated to parties and dinners. Now, I don't concern myself with the purpose of these events but rather their impact on the company. We are still trying to recover from the results of the last quarter, and we've significantly reduced spending on acquiring new clients. This has put us in a difficult position compared to our competitors. You see, monsieur, issues like these are major contributors to business failure, and I wanted to address this matter from the outset before it became a habit."

Marc said, "Well if you say so, but from what I have heard, this was not the first time you both fought."

He smirked, "Monsieur, Qui terre a, guerre a. One who has land has quarrels, and so did we. Our business is quite competitive, and in competition, we might argue occasionally, but that doesn't mean I didn't like her or didn't want to work with her. I liked her a lot; she inspired me to work harder and get better at my job. In the beginning, I was more involved in the technical side of the company's management. After all, I am an engineer first and then an entrepreneur. Then, I realized that to grow this business, I have to be more involved in the business side of it and let more intelligent people handle the technical side of it."

Marc knew what competition he was talking about, but he wanted to dig deeper into him and asked, "Weren't you supposed to be on the same side of this competition? I get the arguments you can have with other companies, but why between yourselves?"

He replied calmly, "To accelerate our growth, we both agreed to acquire new clients separately, and to keep us motivated, we decided to share the profit from the clients we have under our names and the work that the client brings to us."

Marc asked, "So that means whoever has more clients will have more share in the company business?"

He agreed with this statement.

Further, Marc asked, "So, what will happen to all her clients now when she is gone, and what will her profit share be?"

He responded calmly, maintaining his composure, "Yes, I will start handling all her clients now that she is gone, but she was a smart girl. At the start of the company, she nominated her sister Roohi as the beneficiary. So, all the profits that her clients make will go to her sister, and after a certain time, it will be in percentage when our client list grows. I don't know the exact percentage or deal, but I can refer you to my lawyer, and you can get further details from him. Also, her parents have a huge share in this company, so I don't get any money if you are thinking that I have any benefit from her being gone. On the contrary, my workload will be doubled now, and we might have to hire someone to fill her place."

Aware of his competitive nature, Marc attempted to break his composed posture and inquired, "What would have happened if she had split the company and taken all of her clients with her? I have heard she handled more clients than you do?"

Despite his slight irritation, he maintained his composure and replied, "While it's true that Maysa had more clients than me, it doesn't necessarily translate to higher revenue for the company. Whoever provided you with this information is likely not familiar with our company dynamics. In reality, my clients contribute more significantly to our revenue stream. Our disagreements stemmed from Maysa's tendency to overspend despite not matching her earnings. I did consider the possibility of splitting the company once or twice, and I even discussed it with her. However, our longstanding friendship and shared history of hard work prevented me from pursuing that option. Maysa and I built this company together from the ground up, starting as freelancers and gradually expanding our operations. Our first major client marked a significant milestone for us, signaling that our efforts were paying off. While our current office is bigger, our journey began in a much smaller space with only seven employees. Although we've made significant progress, I still believe we have room for improvement. Splitting the company would have jeopardized our stability and potentially led to its closure. If you have doubts about Maysa's intentions, I encourage you to review our quarterly report, which outlines each client's contribution to our revenue."

This new revelation took Marc and Aynaz aback. If Andre was telling the truth, it meant that James might have been lying about Maysa considering splitting the company.

Andre continued, "Yes, we were not on the best terms lately, but that doesn't mean I didn't like her, or we were enemies. We have known each other for a long time and have known each other's families as well. I started this business not for the money but because of my passion. I have money already."

Picking up on his sarcasm, Marc replied wittily, "As you said, you knew each other very well, or maybe a little too well. Yes, it is not always about money; sometimes, it could be something more involved. How is your girlfriend, Claire? She didn't attend the funeral with you. After all, you both knew each other's family for a long time."

Andre grew uneasy with this change of conversation and replied, "Yes, she is doing well. She was not in the city that day so she couldn't come, but she didn't have any problem with Maysa. She did call Sajid and gave her condolences to them."

Curious, Marc asked, "How did you two meet? If you don't mind me asking."

Andre replied with agitation, "She is a model, and we met at one of our promotional events. She was James' friend, and he had introduced her to me."

Marc glanced at Aynaz, silently questioning her thoughts on Claire's possible involvement in the murder.

Andre abruptly interjected, "Sorry, I would have to go now; I have an important meeting to attend. I hope I was of help to you."

Marc responded, "Yes, you were, thank you. Before we leave,

when can we meet Miss Claire?"

"She is in France right now for the fashion show she is working on, and I am not sure of the exact dates she will be back. I apologize; I need to leave now."

"Very well, keep us posted on her return, and pray we don't get any dirt on her. If we do, she won't be participating in any other shows. Also, please inform us before leaving the city.

Marc noticed a sigh of relief on Andre's face as he left the office.

Before departing, Marc and Aynaz entered Maysa's office. It was smaller than Andre's but well-decorated, with an organized desk that made it seem like she would return to work in the morning. There was a dead monitor screen, papers piled up in front of the empty chair, an office cordless phone, some pictures of her parents, sister, and James, a half-empty coffee takeaway cup, and some dust on the oakwood tabletop. The dust and the half-empty coffee mug indicated that her office had yet to be cleaned, which was a good sign for them.

They browsed through the office, examining some files and papers. Numerous numbers and abbreviations didn't make much sense to them. Aynaz then checked the locked drawer on her desk. Utilizing her training, she picked up the lock and found a mobile phone, but it was dead. She discreetly placed it in her purse. Additionally, she discovered a hospital receipt dated almost a month ago, which she handed over to Marc, along with some other papers she deemed relevant to the case.

At that moment, the receptionist entered the office and said, "Désolé, monsieur et madame ne peuvent pas être ici."

Marc replied, "Oui, nous partons," and they left the office premises.

63

Chapter 9:
Marc and Aynaz

It was nearing 7 pm as Marc and Aynaz exited Andre's office. They made a stop at their go-to spot, the Cafeteria on Stanley Street, close to their office in downtown Montreal. Marc opted for his usual black coffee and Montreal bagel, while Aynaz chose Macarons with French vanilla.

Taking their seats in their customary spot near the corner, allowing them a view of the entire cafe, Marc sat silently, lost in his thoughts. Aynaz could sense the weight of the case bearing down on him.

Breaking the silence, she mentioned, "I heard Sydney is coming home from college for the summer vacation."

Marc, returning to the present moment, responded, "Yes, my daughter plans to visit me. Hopefully, I'll have something better to distract me from this case."

As a divorcee with shared custody of his daughter with his ex-wife, Laura, Marc often found himself engrossed in his work, so Sydney mostly spent her summer breaks with her mother. But this year, she was visiting him during the break. While he cherished his time with his daughter, he also felt a responsibility to contribute to making the city safer for families like his by combating crime.

Gazing out at the rain through the window, Marc mused, "Isn't it astonishing how our lives are shaped by the people around us, often without us even realizing it? We become who we are in response to the influences we encounter."

Aynaz, intrigued by this philosophical insight, inquired, "What do you mean?"

He looked at her and responded, "Well, why do you think Maysa and Andre started fighting when they were so close that they started a company together? If they didn't trust each other or were not fond of each other, they wouldn't have made such a big commitment to going into business together. But because of the environment that she got, that is, her parents did not approve of her life choices and getting into fights with her boyfriend, she became this person who started taking out her anger at work and began to share her personal life with a stranger. When she already has good friends like Tracey and Hina, why would she befriend a stranger, let alone share her personal life?"

Aynaz realized that Marc had started to build a soft corner for Maysa and might take this case passionately, being the father of a teenage daughter.

She lightened the mood and said, "Yeah, that is the only reason I spend a lot of time with you, so that I also start saying these philosophical quotes to sound intelligent in front of others."

Marc's face released the tension on his forehead, and he forced a smile.

She continued, "Do you believe what Andre said about their fights, that there were no personal feelings, and it was all professional pressure?"

"Well, with all the history between these two, I won't be surprised to find out that it was a little personal as well, or they were involved with each other in the past. But even if he was jealous or wanted complete control over the company, it doesn't prove that he has anything to do with her death."

She asked, "Then, who do you think is more probable to be the killer?"

The crease on his forehead reappeared, and he replied, "Well, it is hard to say. For all we know, it could be all of them or even none of them."

After a brief pause, he resumed, "There are several potential motives we can explore to narrow down the purpose behind the murder. These typically revolve around Lust, Love, Envy, Fear, or Greed. If we were to consider lust as the primary motive, Rehan would be our primary suspect. However, no clear evidence suggests he had any physical involvement with her or desired it. Additionally, investigations into his call records and activity on matrimonial sites indicate he actively sought a partner for marriage. So, why would he suddenly resort to murder?"

He took a moment, peering into his takeaway coffee cup before continuing, "Considering love as a motive, James could be a suspect due to relationship issues. However, experiencing relationship troubles doesn't necessarily lead to murder unless one is a psychopath. If fear of societal shame was the driving force, then Sajid would be under suspicion. But why now? She had been involved with James for five years, so what prompted him, or perhaps them, to resort to murder at this particular juncture? And if we delve into the motive of greed for power or money, Andre might be considered. Yet, coming from a wealthy background, why would he risk his freedom by resorting to murder?"

Aynaz quickly jotted down notes in her diary and interjected, "So, we've covered Lust, Love, Fear, and Greed. What about Envy?"

"Yes, you are right. More often than we realize, people resort to extreme actions out of jealousy. Whether it's spreading rumors, gossiping, or attempting to harm someone emotionally, jealousy can drive people to do terrible things. But was there someone so consumed by envy that they plotted Maysa's murder? This wasn't a crime of passion; it was a meticulously planned act. Who do you think could have been envious enough of Maysa to resort to murder?"

Aynaz considered for a moment before responding, "Well, I can only think of one person right now: Hina, Maysa's cousin."

Marc was surprised by this suggestion and asked for clarification.

Aynaz referred to her notes and explained, "During Sajid's interrogation, he mentioned that Hina and Maysa were competitive as children. As they grew older, Maysa became more successful than Hina and was in a better position. Additionally, their relationship strained when James entered their lives."

Marc realized that there were still many angles to explore and that he hadn't thoroughly analyzed all potential suspects.

"You're right," he conceded. There's more to this case than meets the eye. I'm almost certain that crucial information is missing. Until we uncover the trigger point for these suspects, all these motives are just speculation. We need to understand why someone who supposedly loved Maysa would resort to such extreme measures."

He continued, "Could you get her mobile phone scanned, which you recovered from her office, and see if we can find anything important there? I will go and check at this hospital tomorrow evening to find out why she reached out to them. Also, please schedule Hina's questioning for tomorrow morning and Tracey's for the day after. We can't leave a stone unturned in this case!"

"While we are talking about leaving no stones unturned, I somehow feel that the problems in their lives started only after James' accident one and a half years ago." Aynaz contributed.

Reflecting on her observation, he responded, "You're right; that was the only common point they didn't disagree on in their interrogations - that their lives changed after that accident. Can you ask Antoine to delve deeper into that incident? Find out what happened, if it was reported, and how it occurred. Thanks."

Aynaz proudly affirmed, "Certainly, sir. You got it."

Chapter 10:

Hina's Interrogation

Marc arrived at the station early the following day, his thoughts still lingering from the previous evening. Stepping into the lookout room adjacent to the interrogation room, he found Hina waiting for him. She appeared nervous, fidgeting with her feet while trying to maintain composure from the waist up. Dressed in a white top and long earrings, she wore minimal makeup.

Taking a seat opposite Hina, Marc was accompanied by Aynaz, who positioned herself in a corner to observe and document the interaction. Marc looked into Hina's eyes and spoke gently, "I don't want to trouble you too much, but I need to ask you some questions, and I hope you'll answer them truthfully to the best of your knowledge."

Hina nodded in acknowledgment.

Marc began, "You and Maysa have been childhood friends, so I assume you knew her quite well. Do you believe she was troubled by anything recently?"

Hina responded, "Yes, I've known her for a long time, almost growing up together. But lately, we haven't been as connected as we used to be. She had a lot going on in her life that I wasn't a part of, so it's inevitable that our connection gradually faded."

Marc inquired, "Even good friends tend to share everything with each other, even if they only talk once a week."

Hina responded, "She made a new friend, so she stopped calling me frequently. When I reached out, our conversations were superficial, mainly about her job. I sensed she was avoiding discussing her personal life with me."

"Why do you think that is?" Marc pressed.

Hina took a deep breath before answering, "About a year ago, after James' accident, his behavior changed. He became envious and possessive. Maysa confided in me more during that time, even sharing concerns about James following her to work. My father had mentioned that Sajid uncle was also worried and wanted her to leave James. So, I suggested she consider leaving him, thinking it was in her best interest."

She paused, her gaze dropping before continuing, "But she misunderstood my intentions, accusing me of discussing her life with her parents behind her back. She felt betrayed, though I only shared what my father told me and never spoke about her to him or Sajid uncle. It led to a quarrel, and she lashed out, implying I couldn't understand because I'd never been in a relationship. It was a personal attack, and I felt humiliated. I retorted that if that was what a relationship entailed, then I wanted no part in it, and I hung up. From then on, we avoided discussing James or her love life."

He further inquired, "Is your father close to your uncle? Did he say anything else about him?"

"They both are first cousins, and he was the reason my father came and settled in Montreal. In our initial days uncle helped us settle our business in Montreal. Also, they both are in the same community, so they meet frequently after daily prayers or some dinners or gatherings at homes."

"My father didn't tell me a lot about what they both talked about, but once I remember he had come to our house for dinner, and after dinner, my father and Sajid uncle went to my father's office to discuss something important. I was in the living room, but I could hear them talking; they thought I was sleeping and didn't care to close the door."

Marc got excited and interrupted, "What did they talk about?"

She rolled her eyes up without moving her head too much. She replied, "Initially, they talked about some work stuff, but then I heard uncle complaining about Maysa and how he is ashamed of the fact that she is dating a non-Muslim man even when he is not good for her at all. He mentioned that she was successful, while he considered James a failure in life. He even insinuated that she could have easily found a better man."

Marc suddenly dropped the excitement and said, "Everyone already knew that Sajid never liked James; what's the news about that?"

She looked towards Marc and said softly, "He went on saying that he hated James to the core as he was the one who had influenced her to do a lot of bad things, including living together before marriage."

Marc sighed with his head.

She continued, "He was more worried about Roohi then."

Marc replied, "What about Roohi?"

She took a moment to respond, her voice measured. "He was worried that Roohi had grown close to Maysa, looking up to her as an independent and successful woman in both education and work. He feared Roohi might follow in her sister's footsteps, possibly entering into a relationship with a non-Muslim man or engaging in other rebellious behavior. Despite his efforts to limit Roohi's interactions with her sister, he couldn't entirely prevent their meetings. Sajid confessed that if Roohi followed the same path, he would consider it a failure in his parenting, attributing it to his own shortcomings."

Marc's realization dawned on him. Sajid's animosity towards James outweighed his concerns about societal perception. His fear of his daughters straying from his teachings fueled his actions.

Turning to Aynaz, Marc voiced his thoughts. "Sajid's intense hatred for James and his fears regarding his daughters might have motivated him to commit a crime. But why target his daughter instead of the person he blames for her supposed corruption?"

Aynaz remained silent, pondering the same question.

After several minutes of tense silence, Aynaz inquired, "You mentioned Maysa had made new friends. Who were you referring to?"

Hina replied, "She befriended Rehan. I played a role in fostering their friendship."

Aynaz pressed for clarification, asking, "How so?"

"After her first encounter with him at a conference, she told me about him and asked me to become friends with him. According to her, we were a good fit together, as he was a single, well-to-do

Indian-origin Muslim man of almost the same age as me in Montreal, which was a very rare find. So, I thought she was right, and there was nothing wrong with just befriending him and seeing where it goes."

Aynaz asked, "So, did she introduce you two?"

"Yes, she did, and we went on a date as well. But afterward, when I messaged him directly, he never responded. I thought he wasn't interested in me, so I dropped that idea. However, later, I found out that she and Rehan got closer."

Aynaz looked at Marc and replied to Hina, "Well, it is not my position to say anything here, but just to let you know, it was Maysa who asked Rehan not to answer your texts. We have gone through their chat history, and we found that. I am sorry; I believe there must be some good reason behind it."

Marc observed silently as he noticed anger flashing in her eyes.

Hina angrily replied, "I always knew she was somehow behind it, and she never could have seen me getting ahead of her in any way. She always wanted to win at everything, even in relationships. She wanted to have a better relationship than me, so she stopped him from answering."

Marc observed a sense of comparison between the two women, but he also realized that this was the first time she had heard about it, so she wouldn't have acted against her for this.

Aynaz further inquired, "Do you think she could have done anything to win against you?"

Hina's expression shifted, reflecting a mix of confusion and disbelief. "After hearing this, I just don't think that I know her anymore."

"So, would you also have done anything to win against her?" Aynaz pressed on, her tone betraying a subtle suspicion.

The implication hit Hina like a sudden blow. She felt the weight of accusation settling upon her, and her voice trembled as she responded, "What? I could never do anything to her. I agree we had some differences, but we were always friends, and I had always admired her for her success and boldness in making her own decisions."

Marc observed the exchange, noting Aynaz's conviction and Hina's genuine distress. He contemplated silently, acknowledging the complexity of the situation. "You see, the small details, like giving an example of what she was proud of, like making her own decisions boldly, indicate to us that she is telling the truth. But of course, I could be wrong, and she might not have done it, but that doesn't mean she doesn't know who did it or had nothing to do with the murder."

Aynaz maintained her steady gaze at Hina as she slowly began to sob. "Why would I kill the only close childhood friend I have?"

Marc interjected, seeking to clarify the investigation's stance. "We are not indicating that you did it, but we have to keep everyone as a suspect until we find the real killer. So, if you know anything that could help us more here, then you should tell us."

"I have told you everything that I know of," Hina insisted through her tears.

"Okay, if you remember anything else, do let us know, and yes, don't leave the town until this investigation is over without telling us first," Marc instructed firmly.

Chapter 11:
Visit to the hospital

Scene 1: The car ride

On the tenth day, since the murder, Marc found himself alone, driving to the hospital referenced on the receipt he had obtained from Maysa's office. Troubled by his lack of progress in identifying the real culprit or culprits, he sifted through all the interactions he had with those close to Maysa. Each person seemed entrenched in their version of events, leaving Marc grappling with uncertainty.

In a moment of introspection, Marc engaged in a monologue with himself.

"When someone recounts a witnessed event, they're not necessarily conveying the absolute truth, but rather their interpretation of it based on their emotions, feelings, and relationships with the individuals involved. Our perception of truth is often colored by subjectivity. This is clearly reflected in the adage that we have heard from our childhood. Love blinds us toward the shortcomings of the person we love the most. This illustrates how our emotions can skew our perception."

"Another common saying is that there are two sides to a coin, that is, there could be more than one version of an event, so it becomes essential to listen to everyone and then conclude, especially in my field of work. For example, one person can be a hero in one's story while a villain in another's. Let us try to think this through, suppose an event happened, let's take a very common example that most of us might have gone through at a certain stage of our life, i.e. breakups."

"If a relationship breaks, there are usually two people involved, and each one tries to assign blame to the other for the demise of their relationship. Both parties recount the same incident but from their own perspectives. For example, one person can say their relationship died because of the other person's lack of commitment, and on the other hand, the other person can blame too much nagging and interference in their relationship by the first person here."

"It becomes challenging to discern the truth because each person is focused on what they perceive was wrong in their relationship, and these perceptions can differ greatly. The complexity arises from the fact that each individual believes they are telling the truth, and they tell their side of the story so convincingly that it becomes hard to identify the real truth. They can recount their version of events with unwavering conviction, without any apparent inconsistencies, as it aligns with their perception of reality."

"Or to put it in simple words, they think that they are telling the truth, and hence it becomes difficult actually to distinguish between the actual truth and the perceived truth."

"So, I believe the truth can be subjective, manipulated, or even wrong. It finally depends on the storyteller's perception. It could be different for different people and all being right or all being wrong at the same time."

"However, it is my responsibility to scrutinize through the narratives and discern the objective truth of the matter, irrespective of personal biases or subjective interpretations."

Scene 2: The hospital

Marc arrived at the hospital and, leveraging his authority as a law enforcer, compelled the receptionist to guide him to the doctor's cabin, where Maysa was consulting.

Addressing the doctor, Marc inquired, "I'm here to understand why Maysa, one of your patients, was seeking consultation. Was she experiencing any health issues?"

The doctor responded, "I'm not authorized to disclose information about other patients; I'm sorry."

With a firm tone, Marc pressed, "Well, your patient was murdered, and I'm the investigator handling her case. Will you cooperate with us, or do I need to bring you in for questioning?"

Taken aback, the doctor replied with shock and compassion, "Oh, I'm sorry to hear that. Maysa was a kind and resilient young woman with a positive outlook on life. I can't fathom who would harm her."

"Yeah, can you please tell me why she visited you?" Marc inquired.

The doctor revealed, "In that case, this might be relevant to your investigation. Maysa was two months pregnant and intended to undergo an abortion. She had scheduled the procedure for this week but failed to show up. I assumed she had a change of heart and decided to keep the baby. The prospect of abortion deeply affected her, and I believe she reconsidered her decision. When asked about her reasons, she insisted it was her personal choice and declined further examination. However, she made it clear that no one was pressuring her into the decision."

Marc was momentarily stunned, absorbing the news without speaking.

The doctor continued, "I hope this information helps."

Gathering his thoughts, Marc asked, "Do you happen to know who the father might be?"

She replied, "Sorry, she had always visited alone, and when I asked her about the father, she replied that it was a mistake and that she wanted to correct it. I couldn't push her to tell her father's name. It is against our policies to make a woman feel comfortable with this procedure."

He inquired further, "Is there anything else that you think can help us?"

"Not sure if this will help, but she was going through a lot of stress in her life. She was taking 2mg of Xanax regularly, which is a heavy dose that normally people consume when fighting with anxiety, depression or similar problems."

Marc felt a pang of sadness upon hearing this revelation. He couldn't help but wonder how Maysa had so many people around her—family and friends—yet no one seemed close enough to realize her pain or to whom she could confide. What troubled him even more was the fact that not a single person had mentioned the pregnancy in their interrogations.

A whirlwind of thoughts flooded Marc's mind. Did nobody know about Maysa's pregnancy, and she kept it to herself? Was her death indeed a suicide, as initially suspected? Had he misinterpreted the case entirely, given Maysa's struggles with anxiety and the burden of concealing an abortion? Was he the victim of his own emotions, categorizing this case as a murder when it could potentially be a suicide?

"I need to get my thoughts organized to solve this case," Marc resolved.

He thanked the doctor and left the consultation room, his mind racing with unanswered questions.

Chapter 12:
Marc's Turmoil and The Medical Report

Having mulled over the possibility that Marc might have been chasing a ghost, considering the potential of this being a suicide case all along, he found himself uneasy with the thought.

Marc knocked on Aynaz's office door, an unusual occurrence as he rarely sought her out directly unless troubled by persistent thoughts.

Surprised by Marc's visit, Aynaz welcomed him with a calm smile and gestured for him to enter. Her office was modest, with a desk, chairs, and a towering pile of papers in one corner, hinting at the weight of their caseload.

As Marc stepped inside and closed the door behind him, Aynaz met his gaze and inquired, "How can I assist you, Marc?"

"I'm grappling with this case. It's been nearly two weeks without a breakthrough. Do you think we're on the right track?" Marc voiced his concern.

Reflecting on their previous discussions, Aynaz responded thoughtfully, "Our analysis of the case through the lens of five main motives—lust, love, envy, greed, and fear—has provided some insight into potential suspects and motives. However, there may be other factors at play, such as anger, hatred, or selfishness. Despite this, I believe we're making progress in narrowing down the list of suspects."

He replied, "Anger, hatred, or selfishness are feelings, and people do commit crimes when they have strong emotions like these, but this doesn't necessarily provide them with motives. We need to understand why someone hates her or is angry at her, and these questions can be classified into the five motives that I listed before."

Aynaz realized the significance of his words. A person's emotions could stem from motives like love, jealousy, or greed, and she said, "So, basically, all feelings can be attributed to these five main motives."

Glancing at the pile of papers in the corner, he asked, "But what I meant to ask was, do you think my initial evaluation that this was a murder and not a suicide case was correct? What if she was under too much stress because of all the things going on in her life, and she just wanted to end her suffering?"

Finally understanding his dilemma, she replied, "We didn't follow your evaluation solely because of your instinct but because of the observations you made at the murder scene. Why would a person order a burger from a restaurant and then add poison to their tea or invite a friend before they kill themselves? And what about the missing cup? It makes more sense that she was killed and didn't plan on killing herself."

He contemplated, "What if she was depressed and suddenly decided to end her own life to escape her misery?"

She calmly responded, "I was just about to inform you that we have finally received the autopsy report this morning. There was a fire at the hospital in Toronto, which delayed its arrival, but fortunately, it wasn't destroyed in the fire."

Handing him the autopsy report, she waited for his response.

The report revealed that the victim's body showed no signs of physical harm or sexual activity. However, her left middle fingernail was missing, which stood out against her otherwise well-maintained nails. The time of death was estimated to be around 5:00 PM on March 17th, with the cause being poison ingested through a beverage, as indicated by traces found in the teacup. The specific poison identified was Ricin.

Aynaz, intrigued by the details, inquired about the poison's nature, prompting Marc to share his knowledge. He explained that Ricin originates from Castor beans, easily accessible and extractable from the residue left after Castor oil extraction. Notably, Ricin is highly toxic and soluble, making it an effective poison for food or drink contamination. Marc emphasized that it is also considered a poison of terror as it is cheap and easily extracted, there is no vaccine or treatment for this poison, it is very poisonous, and it can also be converted into a gaseous form to terrorize the public.

Realizing the calculated nature of the poisoning, Aynaz questioned whether it could be deemed a suicide. However, Marc concurred that the intricate planning and knowledge required to extract and administer Ricin indicated premeditated murder, aligning with his initial assessment upon reviewing the autopsy report.

Marc stated, "I think you've already read it in the report; she was pregnant. I visited her doctor yesterday and found out, but the doctor didn't know who the father was. Additionally, she was taking a high dose of Xanax, indicating she was battling anxiety."

Aynaz, frustrated, responded, "Who could blame her for being depressed? With a jealous boyfriend, envious cousin, greedy colleague, and a disapproving father, anyone could get depressed, not to mention the unplanned baby."

Marc analyzed, "Now, at least we know the trigger point for this murder. It was the news of her impending motherhood, but no one mentioned this in their interrogations. Either none of them knew about it, or someone is trying to conceal their knowledge, which might have led to her murder."

He continued, "So, we can hypothesize that if the baby was Rehan's, then James might have discovered it and killed her due to his possessive nature and unrequited love."

Aynaz proposed, "Or perhaps Sajid learned about the baby and killed her out of fear for his reputation and the potential impact on his other daughter."

Marc added, "Or it could have been Rehan when he realized his feelings couldn't be reciprocated upon learning about the baby with James. Moreover, we already have a witness who saw him at the murder site."

Aynaz remarked, "Knowing who the father of the baby was could offer valuable insight."

Marc agreed, "Or if we knew who knew about this news and tried to hide it from us, that could also lead us to a suspect."

As they pondered their theories, Antoine knocked and entered the cabin. "I just received the call and chat records from her office phone."

Excitedly, Marc inquired, "Did you find anything important?"

Antoine reported, "There are mostly professional calls and chats, but there's one chat with Tracey discussing her pregnancy. She asked Tracey not to tell James or anyone else about it, which was dated almost one month back."

Mark exclaimed, "Tracey! After hearing about her story, I never considered that she could be connected with the murder."

He glanced at Aynaz and continued, "I know everyone should be considered a suspect until we identify the real culprit, but sometimes we have to go with our gut feelings. Anyways, can I read the chat?"

Antoine handed the papers to Marc.

Marc remarked, "So, she did mention the pregnancy, but she hasn't disclosed the abortion. At least not in this chat. There's a possibility she may have confided in James or Hina. It's unlikely she would have told Sajid or Rehan, as they seem unrelated. However, Hina could have informed Sajid, who might have reacted by killing her. This also explains why he might have targeted her instead of James; her being pregnant even after James's death would tarnish his image."

Aynaz inquired, "Does the chat mention who the father is?"

Marc replied, "No, it doesn't. But the absence of mention doesn't imply she didn't disclose it personally. We need to interrogate Tracey to determine why she hasn't mentioned the pregnancy to them yet and if Maysa told her about the father."

"I believe we're close to uncovering the culprit and finally achieving justice for her."

With a calm mind and a clear plan of action, Marc left the cabin, stating, "I don't think anyone can ever truly attain justice for her, but we'll do our utmost to find the murderer."

Chapter 13:
Tracey's Interrogation

Aynaz entered Marc's office the next day, her expression grave with the weight of pressing matters.

"It's been a week since we arrested Rehan," she began, her voice tinged with urgency. "We can't keep him in custody unless we press charges against him. His lawyer is threatening to sue us for the alleged malpractice of power by a law enforcer."

Marc nodded grimly. "Yeah, we have to release him. We don't have anything substantial against him."

Marc continued, shifting gears to another pressing issue. "When is Tracey scheduled for questioning?"

"That was also on my mind," she replied, her brow furrowing in thought. "I was thinking, instead of calling her to the station, we should give her a surprise visit. Currently, everyone believes our prime suspect is Rehan, and we're gathering evidence against him. If we call her here, she'd come prepared. I want to observe her reactions when we question her about pregnancy."

After a moment's consideration, he made his decision. "I'm sold on the idea. Let me grab my coat, and we'll pay her a visit. Do you have the address?"

She prompted, "She lives near the Snowden metro station.

Around 20 mins drive from here."

Marc's interest was piqued. "Interesting! It's merely a ten to fifteen-minute drive from Maysa's apartment on Ridgewood Avenue."

*****

Aynaz knocked on Tracey's apartment door, situated on the third floor of a weathered, old building. Marc, catching his breath from climbing the stairs due to the non-functional lift, struggled with his health, exacerbated by his increased smoking habits brought on by stress and overthinking.

The building's proximity to the subway station offered convenient transportation access. However, the condition of the building suggested it was likely a low-cost rental apartment complex.

As a professional dancer, Tracey's income fluctuated, with periods of plentiful performances followed by lean months, particularly in January after the holiday season. Financial instability compounded by inflation further strained her situation.

Startled by the unannounced visitors, Tracey maintained composure honed from countless stage performances as she greeted Aynaz and Marc at the door.

"Ms. Aynaz and Mr. Marc, what a surprise! Is there anything I can help you with?" Tracey inquired calmly.

"We were just passing through the neighborhood, so we

thought of stopping by," Aynaz replied.

Marc interjected, "Do you mind if we come inside? We would like to ask some questions related to Maysa."

Tracey extended a welcoming invitation, "Sure, why not? Please come in."

Marc entered the apartment. It looked like Maysa's apartment but only a little older. As they entered, there was a living area with two two-seater sofas and a coffee table. Half of the living space was vacant; probably, she left it like that for her practices. It was a one-bedroom small apartment but was nicely décor-ed. As Marc walked through the hallway, he noticed a twelve-foot winter boot in the shoe, which looked like a men's shoe.

They sat on the sofa. Tracey offered to get them coffee, but they insisted not to.

Tracey asked, "So, how can I help you?"

Marc asked him, "Let's start by telling us what you were doing on 17th March around 5 pm?"

She replied, "It was St. Patrick's Day, and I had an event to perform. So, I was busy the entire day."

Aynaz interrupted her, "If I remember correctly, your performance was in the evening from 7 pm onwards."

She realized they had come prepared, but continuing with her calmness, she replied, "Yes, but we need to practice before the actual performance, so I was rehearsing."

Marc, in a grim voice, asked her, "Out of all her friends, you had not texted or called her that day. Do you feel bad about not talking to your friend that day?"

She looked into his eyes and replied, "As I said, I was busy rehearsing as it was my first big gig of the year, so I wanted to perform well in it. I didn't have much time to call her that day or meet her in a couple of weeks, but I did invite her to the play, and we were supposed to meet after the play. I do feel bad about not being able to talk to her."

He altered his tone, adopting a more cautious approach as he inquired, "Is there anything troubling Maysa may have confided in you? Any issues she was facing?"

In response, she relayed, "Nothing out of the ordinary comes to mind at the moment. She did mention enjoying flirting with Rehan and considering a serious relationship with him, expressing dissatisfaction with James. However, she didn't seem distressed while sharing this. In fact, it appeared she was having fun with Rehan while still dating James. However, she did mention earlier that Rehan wasn't pleased with her relationship with James and wanted her to end it."

Aynaz and Marc exchanged surprised glances at her revelation. They were already aware of Maysa's recent disclosure about her pregnancy, yet she had omitted this detail. This omission raised suspicions in their minds, prompting Marc to proceed with caution in his questioning.

Carefully, Marc inquired, "Did James know about her intention to leave him?"

She responded, "No, James is a kind person. While their relationship wasn't at its peak, he wouldn't have harbored ill thoughts toward her."

Meeting her gaze directly, Marc pressed on, "We received Maysa's autopsy report yesterday, which indicated she was pregnant. Did she ever mention this to you?"

Her eyes widened slightly, and she stumbled over her words for the first time, hastily replying, "No, she never mentioned it to me. I apologize for my reaction; I'm simply taken aback by this news."

Marc refrained from revealing their knowledge of her prior awareness and attempted to exert pressure subtly, stating, "Understandable. However, do you know who won't be surprised by this news? The perpetrator, as they could now be facing charges of double homicide, potentially resulting in life imprisonment or even the death penalty."

Aynaz understood that Marc was attempting to extract information from Tracey.

Tracey, still with a stuttering voice, replied, "Yeah, definitely. That should be the least her killer should be punished with."

Marc noticed a change in Tracey's facial expression, observing that she could no longer maintain her calm demeanor. She began playing with her fingers, displaying signs of nervousness.

Further probing, Marc asked, "Did you know if she was depressed lately or experiencing any anxiety? Considering everything Hina has told us about what Maysa has done for you, you must have taken good care of her?"

Tracey responded, "Yeah, we were very old friends, and over time, our bond has only grown stronger. So, if she was going through something like that, she would have mentioned it to me, but she never did. I know she was not very happy lately, and with the work pressure she had, being as competitive as she was, but I don't think she was depressed or experiencing any anxiety."

While Marc sensed that Tracey was telling the truth, he prodded further, "The report states that she was taking Xanax, a medication to combat anxiety."

This revelation surprised Tracey, and she said, "It never felt that way. Whenever we met, we would discuss my performances, her work achievements, her relationships, her aspirations, etc., besides general topics like movies, fashion, and world news. It never occurred to me that she was going through all that."

Aynaz interjected, asking, "Why do you think she would have hidden this significant news from you when you were quite close to her?"

Tracey replied, "Well, I'm not sure. We used to share everything, but if she had hidden this from me, there must have been a reason behind it."

Aynaz further inquired, "Maybe lately she felt you were not as close as you appear to be with her? or that you have changed?"

Without directly addressing the question, Tracey apologized, citing a forthcoming work meeting as her reason for needing to leave promptly.

Marc seized the opportunity to pose a crucial query before their departure, probing, "Do you know who could have been the father of her baby?"

Tracey paused, considering her response before tentatively suggesting, "I am not sure, but it could be Rehan's."

Aynaz interjected with a reminder of the gravity of such an

accusation against the deceased, cautioning, "This is a very serious accusation on your dead best friend's character."

She then turned to Marc, suggesting a potential motive, "But if the baby was Rehan's, then this gives James a purpose for killing her, don't you think?"

Interrupting the speculation, Tracey swiftly retracted her statement, admitting, "No, I was wrong. It couldn't be Rehan's as she never told me about sleeping with him. I just assumed it might have been him, as she was being very friendly with him and even meeting him frequently. So, it should have been James' child."

Marc, acknowledging her correction, proceeded with one final inquiry: "One last question before we leave: Do you think she would have told this to anyone, maybe James, Rehan, or Hina?"

Tracey reflected, "Maybe to James as it was his child, but I don't think she would have told Hina or Rehan, being she hadn't even told me about that."

Marc smiled at her and said, "Thanks for your cooperation, but please don't leave the town without prior notification, and do reach out if you remember anything else that could be important."

Marc and Aynaz departed, the latter observing a sense of relief on Tracey's countenance.

*****

After settling into the car, Aynaz broke the silence, her tone edged with skepticism. "She was lying through her teeth."

He nodded in agreement, his expression mirroring her doubt. "She lied to us about not knowing about the pregnancy, despite the fact that we have evidence she messaged her about it. Plus, they met soon after to discuss it."

"Yeah," Aynaz chimed in, her frustration evident. "She even tried to fabricate a story about the child's father. And did you notice how relieved she seemed when we left her apartment?"

"Yeah, catching her off guard was a good move. She clearly wasn't expecting us to know about the baby," he remarked.

Aynaz leaned forward, her brow furrowed with concern, "So, how do we proceed from here? If she's involved in the murder, she's not going to confess easily. She remained remarkably composed throughout our questioning and only showed emotion when we really pressed her."

"It's going to be tough to crack her," he admitted. "If we could understand her motive, it might give us some leverage."

Aynaz nodded in agreement. "I don't think she ever intended to leave the apartment. She just wanted us out of there."

"Exactly," he agreed, his gaze lingering on the apartment building as they drove away from the parking lot. "I also noticed a man's boot in the apartment, but we can't jump to conclusions. It's going to be hard to determine whose it was."

He glanced at Aynaz before continuing, "Can you do one thing?"

"Of course," she replied, focusing her attention entirely on what he was going to say.

"Can you go and keep the mobile that we recovered from her

office back in her drawer? But don't lock the drawer. We also need to see if there is any camera covering her office or the area near her office. I believe she thinks that we haven't yet found her phone."

Aynaz exclaimed, "Yes, that makes sense. If she is guilty, then she would try to remove the evidence that could point towards her, and then we can catch her red-handed."

"It would still be hard to gather evidence against her," Marc added.

After driving a mile, he said, "I think she has something to do with James. She was trying to save him when you pointed out that if the baby was Rehan's, then he could be the suspect. Then she changed her statement about Rehan being the father."

"You are right. We also notice their proximity during the funeral gathering. We should see if there was another love triangle in this story that we didn't know about."

Chapter 14:
Antoine's Breakthrough

Aynaz sat in her office, savoring her morning coffee and reflecting on her recent interaction with Tracey. The suspicion lingered in her mind; she couldn't shake the feeling that Tracey might be involved in Maysa's murder. However, her thoughts were interrupted by the sudden chaos erupting in the police station. People busted in and out of the chief's office, creating an atmosphere of disorder.

Curious, Aynaz rushed out of her office and spotted Antoine inside the chief's office. Sensing something significant was happening, she turned to a coworker standing nearby and inquired about the commotion.

"What's going on? Why is there so much chaos today?" Aynaz asked, her voice tinged with urgency.

Her coworker replied, "Haven't you heard? Antoine cracked the murder case from Ridgewood Avenue a couple of weeks ago. The chief called him in to discuss the details."

Realizing that the discussion likely pertained to her and Marc's case, Aynaz felt a surge of astonishment. She couldn't tear her gaze away from Antoine as he conversed with the chief.

Pointing to a table in the corner of the room, her coworker

continued, "Also, we missed out on investigating an old case, so Antoine's been leading that investigation too. He was just in the chief's office. I'm not sure what transpired, but he didn't look as pleased then as he does now. You know how it reflects on the department's image."

Concerned, Aynaz inquired, "Does Marc know about this?"

Her coworker shrugged. "Not sure, but he's in his office."

Confusion clouded Aynaz's thoughts as she struggled to comprehend the situation. The last breakthrough she remembered was the interrogation with Tracey. She couldn't help but wonder if Tracey had confessed or if Antoine had uncovered compelling evidence against her.

She rushed into Marc's office, breathless with urgency, and exclaimed, "Did you hear about it?"

Marc, sitting in his chair looking bewildered, replied, "Yeah, Antoine cracked the case and is claiming that Sajid murdered her daughter."

Her scream reverberated through the office, "What!!"

Quickly adjusting her tone, she continued, "But it was supposed to be Tracey or maybe Rehan or James?"

"Yeah, I know, but he has some key information that points towards him, and this should shock you again, but please try not to shout this time," Marc cautioned.

Embarrassed, she nodded in agreement.

"Do you remember that James had an accident last year in which he narrowly escaped death and was badly wounded? Well,

I had asked Antoine to look into it again as it was coming out to be the common point in everyone's story."

She nodded again, indicating her recollection.

"He found out that it was an attempt to murder, and Sajid was behind that accident."

Her voice rose in disbelief, "What!"

Marc shot her a stern glance.

Correcting herself, she asked softly, "How was Sajid behind it?"

"James was preparing for a long-awaited role, but he had to travel to Ontario for that. Sajid came to know about it as Maysa had asked Sajid if Roohi could stay with her for a couple of days. Sajid then hired someone to loosen his car brakes so that it wouldn't be effective on the highway at high speeds."

"We have caught that person, and he is in custody now. He confessed that Sajid had asked him to do that for money. Antoine found out in the case report that James' insurance company submitted that the brakes were not working properly, so the accident happened. They even tried to sue the car company for making a faulty brake. However, the company confirmed that the brakes were working fine the last time the car was brought in for servicing, and it was documented as well and signed by James. So, the case never opened, and everyone assumed that the brake would have gone bad after the servicing."

"Antoine pointed out that the brake shoes are very sturdy and cannot go bad in just three months unless there is some Formula One racer driving the car. He investigated how the brake could fail in just three months and found out that it could happen only if someone deliberately did it. He then reached out to his sources and caught the man who did it. He did a good job of finding this out, and that's why everyone is praising him, and he is in the chief's office."

She momentarily thought and asked, "But that still didn't confirm that Sajid was behind her killing as well?"

"Yeah, there is no direct proof of that unless he confesses, but it does make a strong case against him by attempting to kill her boyfriend."

"How so?" she inquired.

"He has a statement from Hina that he was really worried about his stature in society, and it was getting depleted because of her, not to mention that he was also worried that his second daughter could follow in her footsteps, which would mean he has failed as a father. So, when he would have found out that she was pregnant before marriage, then that might have triggered that sense of losing, and he would have planned to kill her."

"Also, an attempt to murder indicates that a person is capable of killing someone. Not all people possess that ability." He continued after a slight pause, "To be honest, I am a little relieved that we have found the culprit. This case had started to take a toll on me."

After his remark, a heavy silence hung in the room for some time.

Marc looked at Aynaz and thought to himself, "It is a strange feeling that you have been investigating a case for so long, and you get attached to a case such that even if someone gives you a solution to that case, your mind isn't ready to accept it. At least not until you find out by yourself who the culprit is or make the solution tallies with your investigation. If she would have come up with the same conclusion then her mind wouldn't have questioned it that much and would have accepted it."

After pondering for a while, Aynaz inquired, "But what about Tracey's statement from yesterday?"

Marc replied, "She might have been protecting her friend's reputation by withholding the truth, or perhaps she wished to avoid involvement in the investigation. Knowing about the pregnancy doesn't necessarily implicate her in the murder."

Seating herself across from Marc, Aynaz continued to contemplate.

Several minutes passed before she spoke again, "The entire assumption that Sajid killed Maysa hinges on the belief that he knew about her pregnancy and acted on it. But so far, there's no evidence to support that he was aware of it. If we can establish that he didn't know about the pregnancy, then we can't accuse him."

Marc met her gaze directly, questioning, "Why do you want to do that? Let me ask you a question: what if he did kill her?"

He looked out through the window and said, "I know it's tough to see the case you've been working so hard on solved by someone else, taking away all your efforts. But this is part of life. Not everything is fair, and we should be wise enough to choose our battles."

She took a moment to understand him and replied in a deep and confident tone, "Well, this is the fight I want to pursue, even if you don't. I'm not trying to save Sajid here, but I'm determined to find the real killer and bring justice to Maysa. And if I'm wrong, then maybe I'll discover that Sajid did know about the pregnancy and killed her."

"Have we already arrested him, and has he confessed to either of the crimes?" he inquired.

"Not yet. We're still working on obtaining the arrest warrant," he replied.

After years of working together, he understood her thought process and added, "It might take a couple of hours before we secure the warrant as the commissioner is unavailable."

She then asked, "Will you come with me?"

He shook his head, responding, "No, this is your intuition, and I respect that. It's better if you go alone. I'll text you when we're ready to arrest him. Please be safe. If you encounter any trouble, just text me, and I'll be there in no time."

"Very well. Here goes nothing," she said, then swiftly left his office, her pace doubled from when she entered.

Chapter 15:
Sajid's Home Visit

She stood before Sajid's house, pondering her approach to questioning him. All she needed to ascertain was whether he knew about the pregnancy or not. As far as she knew, she hadn't electronically informed anyone about the pregnancy except Tracey. It was highly unlikely that she had told him. So, either Sajid had learned from another source or Tracey had disclosed it to him.

She knocked on the door.

Najma opened the door and was surprised to see her. "What are you doing here?" she asked bluntly.

Quickly correcting herself, she added, "I mean, how can I help you? Were we supposed to meet today? I remember we had discussed everything during the interrogation."

"Yes, you have. I was just in the neighborhood, so I thought of dropping by to see how you guys are doing. Being a daughter myself, I can understand the pain."

Najma's concerned expression didn't change, but she invited her in.

As they walked through the lobby, Najma announced Aynaz's presence. Sajid was seated in his armchair, gazing at his mobile phone. Aynaz settled onto an L-shaped navy-blue sofa opposite Sajid.

He casually inquired, "Have you found our daughter's killer?" inwardly noting, "Words that should never escape any father's lips."

"Not yet. We are still investigating," she replied.

"Is there something specific you want to inquire about then?"

"Nothing like that; as you can see, I came here alone and not with Marc. Please consider this as an informal visit being a daughter myself, I understand your pain right now. So, I thought of visiting you to see if you both were doing alright."

Najma felt a pang of remorse upon hearing her, but Sajid knew it was never what they said it was.

Sajid's response was sarcastic, "Well, in that case, thank you for gracing us with your presence during this time of grief. We're managing as any grieving parents would. Your sympathy is unnecessary; what we need is justice for our daughter."

Aynaz met his gaze, recognizing his unyielding stance. She inquired softly, "And how is Roohi? Is she coping well?"

"Roohi is currently at school," Najma replied, seeking to maintain the conversation.

Attempting to delve deeper, she continued, "I heard Maysa had a disagreement with Hina over Rehan. It seems they weren't on speaking terms."

Acknowledging Maysa's complexities, Sajid reflected, "Our daughter made mistakes, but she possessed a kind heart. Whatever conflicts arose, I believe she would have forgiven them. Hina and Tracey were both dear to her, and they had shared a bond since childhood. While Hina was a constant presence, Tracey gradually became closer."

Interrupting, Najma offered her perspective, "While Maysa maintained strong ties with both, I believe her relationship with Hina was more competitive. Tracey, however, offered unwavering support, particularly in Maysa's career pursuits. Given the circumstances, she might have leaned towards Tracey. But Maysa never treated them differently."

She inquired, "I see. Do you happen to know if either of them was proficient in biology or botany?"

He responded, "I doubt Tracey was particularly focused on academics. Her aspirations leaned more towards dancing. However, Hina was diligent in her studies."

Swiftly changing the subject, she asked, "Given our religious beliefs against premarital physical relationships, and assuming you instilled the same values in her, why do you think Maysa might have disregarded this?"

He lowered his gaze before replying, "No matter the guidance provided during adolescence, one cannot predict their child's choices in adulthood. Maysa was no exception. She succumbed to James's influence, a day I regret deeply. Despite my efforts to intervene, I couldn't sever their connection."

Noting his animosity towards James, she observed a stark contrast to his feelings for his daughter.

Attempting to provoke further, she ventured, "While James may have influenced her, Maysa was no longer a child when he entered her life. Shouldn't she bear equal responsibility for her decisions?"

He replied, "I know what you are trying to do here. You are trying to provoke me so that I will say something that will help you in this case. But trust me, we have told you everything that we knew about that day or her life. To answer your question, I don't think it was her fault at all. It was only and only because of James. Hasn't he told you how he used to follow her to the office and stalk her and try to win over her after they first met? He did everything he could to pursue her, and only if I had known at that time, I would have stopped it."

She replied, "No, I'm not trying to provoke you. But how did you find out that James used to follow her? Did Maysa herself tell you about this?"

"After she started dating him, she became more reserved with us. It was Hina who informed her about James's following of our daughter."

Aynaz noted their close relationship with Hina and reasoned that if Hina knew about the pregnancy, she might have disclosed it to them.

Digging deeper, she asked, "And what about Tracey? Did she ever mention anything about their relationship?"

Sajid's tone grew heavy with annoyance. "No, we weren't as close to Tracey. Hina, being my cousin's daughter, visited us frequently. But yes, once Hina mentioned that Tracey had feelings for James initially. I wish he had chosen Tracey instead of our daughter."

Shocked by this revelation, Aynaz remained composed. "I understand. Do you think Tracey would have confided in Hina about Maysa if she had shared something with Tracey but not with Hina?"

Sajid's irritation peaked. "What exactly do you want to know? Quit beating around the bush and ask directly. You came here unannounced, pretending to care. I know you have an agenda, so just ask. I'm willing to tell you anything to solve this case but stop with the games."

Aynaz received a text from Marc: "Got the warrant. Leave immediately. OTW."

She wasted no time in responding: "Okay, I will say bluntly then, Maysa was pregnant when she died, and so we are trying to see if anyone knew about it or if this had anything to do with the murder."

Najma's reaction was immediate and visceral; she burst into tears. Sajid, on the other hand, remained stoic, his gaze fixed on the ground. Seeing his reaction, Aynaz thought he already knew about it, but then Sajid placed his left hand over his chest and came down to the floor. Acting swiftly, Najma instructed Aynaz to fetch water while she rushed to administer Sajid's medication before calling for an ambulance.

As Aynaz tended to Sajid, Najma revealed his heart condition and explained how shock or distress could trigger an attack. Aynaz realized that Sajid's collapse indicated his ignorance of Maysa's pregnancy, adding another layer of shock to the situation.

Expressing her apologies and concern, Aynaz acknowledged the gravity of her actions and their impact on Najma and Sajid. Despite her guilt, she emphasized the importance of uncovering the truth.

She called up Marc from her car before driving off, "Hello Marc, I need you to trust me on this. I believe Sajid didn't kill his daughter, it was someone else."

"Nevertheless, we still need to lock him up for James' accident as that is proven," Aynaz asserted.

"Yes, I understand, but we can't arrest him right now. I informed him about her pregnancy, and it came as a shock, leading to a heart attack. Don't worry. An ambulance has arrived and stabilized him, and we will be taking him to the hospital for further treatment," she explained urgently.

Marc's voice rose in disbelief. "What on earth did you do?"

"Trust me, this is for the best. If we arrest him now, it could worsen the situation," Aynaz replied calmly.

"Alright, I'll inform the chief. But I can only delay the arrest by one day, no more," Marc conceded reluctantly.

"That should suffice. I'm heading to Hina's place. You should come too, and we can discuss further," Aynaz suggested.

After a brief pause, Marc agreed. "I'll be there in 20 minutes."

Chapter 16:
Aynaz's Intuition

Aynaz paced restlessly outside Hina's apartment building, eagerly awaiting Marc's arrival. As Marc pulled over and approached her, she couldn't contain her excitement.

"Marc, I have news for you," Aynaz exclaimed. "That's why I asked you to delay his arrest."

Marc's demeanor remained calm as he responded, "Take a deep breath and tell me."

Aynaz quickly divulged the details of her recent meeting. "Firstly, he seemed genuinely shocked about the pregnancy. When I informed him, he suffered a heart attack and was rushed to the hospital. No one could fake a heart attack that convincingly. Secondly, I discovered that Hina wasn't just close to Maysa, she also maintained contact with Sajid, updating him on Maysa's life after their estrangement. Thirdly, the most crucial piece of information is that Tracey initially had feelings for James. However, upon witnessing his growing closeness to Maysa, she refrained herself from pursuing him."

Marc absorbed the information thoughtfully. "So, Tracey had feelings for James. This connection fills in a gap in the triangle, potentially shedding light on the motive behind the murder. But loving someone doesn't make a person capable of murder."

Aynaz nodded in agreement. "That's why I came here directly—to confirm if Tracey still harbors feelings for James."

"Good work, Aynaz," Marc commended.

Together, they took the elevator to the fourth floor and knocked on Hina's door.

Hina greeted them with surprise. "Hey! What brings you here? You could have just asked me to come down to the station."

Aynaz thought to herself with a smirk, "Lately, I seem to be shocking everyone I meet."

She continued, "No, we were just in the neighborhood, so we thought of stopping by. We need to ask a few questions."

Hina welcomed them inside and gestured for them to take a seat in the hall.

Aynaz got straight to the point. "Last time, we asked you to tell us everything you know about Maysa or anything that could help us solve this mystery."

Hina nodded in understanding. "Yes, I shared everything I knew about her or anything relevant to the case."

Marc interjected, "Then why did you fail to mention that Tracey had feelings for James?"

Hina appeared perplexed. "I suppose it slipped my mind. At the time, I didn't think it was pertinent, considering it was in the past when Tracey confided in me."

Marc pressed further, "Did anything change after that? Did you notice any odd behavior from Tracey?"

"No," Hina replied. "She never mentioned it again. However, now that I think about it, I did observe that she distanced herself, particularly when James and Maysa were together. Although, this could have been coincidental, as she seemed fine before that."

Marc exchanged a glance with Aynaz. "We're still trying to piece things together."

Aynaz turned her attention back to Hina. "Is there anything else you know about them that you haven't shared? Please, think carefully."

Hina paused and rolled her eyes to look at the ceiling and recalled a recent interaction, "Not long ago, I had dinner with Maysa and James. Out of the blue, James asked if Tracey was seeing someone. I assumed he was trying to set her up. Also, I'm not sure if this is relevant, but since Maysa's passing, I've noticed James and Tracey spending a lot of time together. I saw them dining alone at a restaurant recently."

Marc responded, his tone earnest, "Yes, every detail matters, no matter how small."

Hina's expression eased, and she continued, "There's something else I recall, though I initially dismissed it as insignificant. It doesn't involve James or Tracey."

Encouraged, Marc urged, "Please, tell us everything you remember."

"I once spotted Sajid and Rehan chatting in a coffee shop," Hina revealed. "It caught me off guard at the time, but I didn't dwell on it. This happened about a year ago, shortly after my date with Rehan."

The revelation hit Marc and Aynaz like a thunderbolt, causing

Marc to feel as though the ground was slipping from beneath him.

For what felt like an eternity, silence enveloped them as they processed the implications. Their assumptions about Rehan and Sajid's lack of acquaintance shattered.

Finally, Aynaz broke the silence, her voice trembling slightly. "Did you ever inquire about their connection?"

Hina shook her head. "No, I never had the chance to speak with Rehan again after our first date.

And it felt awkward to broach the topic with Sajid uncle."

"Thank you for sharing this with us," Marc said, his gratitude evident. "We must leave now, but please reach out if you remember anything else."

She nodded. "I'll do whatever I can to help catch the culprit."

As they descended to the ground floor, the tension remained palpable.

*****

Outside her apartment building, Aynaz and Marc mulled over the latest developments in the case.

"I'm feeling lost again. Do you think Sajid is really the one who killed his daughter?" Aynaz questioned, her uncertainty palpable.

Marc's gaze shifted to the ground as he replied, "There's definitely something suspicious about Sajid's involvement here, and Rehan doesn't seem as innocent as he portrays himself to be."

And continued with a pause, "Neither of them shared this information that they knew each other from before."

Aynaz pondered aloud, "But why would Sajid meet with Rehan? Now that he's hospitalized, we've lost our chance to question him."

"It's frustrating. It seems like every time we get close to solving this mystery, it slips through our fingers," Marc lamented.

Aynaz retrieved her diary and began listing the known facts. "Let's review what we've gathered so far,

Maysa was pregnant, likely with James' child.

Tracey had feelings for James.

Rehan was flirting with Maysa.

Rehan was present at the crime scene on the day of the murder.

Sajid and Najma were the first to report the murder.

Sajid had a prior acquaintance with Rehan, which he concealed.

Sajid disapproved of Maysa's relationship with James.

James had suspicions about Maysa and would follow her.

James and Tracey appear to be romantically involved now."

Marc replied thoughtfully, "If Sajid had prior knowledge of the murder, he wouldn't have accompanied Najma to her apartment that day, let alone with Roohi."

She panted and asked, "So, you mean Sajid and Rehan might not be involved in the murder?"

Marc responded cautiously, "Sajid may not be, but I can't vouch for Rehan."

She pressed further, "And what about Tracey and James?"

"In his interrogation, James seemed delusional; he denied all the issues in their relationship. As for Tracey, it appears she's the one benefiting most from Maysa's demise."

She speculated, "Perhaps Sajid saw Maysa's death as a way to prevent Roohi from following her sister's path."

"You can't be certain of that. Besides, I believe Sajid's concern for Maysa stemmed from genuine parental love towards her daughter. I doubt he'd resort to such extremes."

She countered firmly, "I hear what you are saying, but I think your perspective might be biased as a father. It could cloud your judgment regarding Sajid."

Marc accepted this accusation somewhere, so he didn't take offense and nodded.

He continued, "To confirm our suspicions, we'll need to question Rehan about his connection to Sajid."

She mused, "We'll need a better pretext than simply being in the neighborhood this time."

A smirk played on Marc's lips before they drove off, plotting their next move.

Chapter 17:
Rehan's House Inspection

Marc and Aynaz stood outside Rehan's apartment, knocking on the door repeatedly, but received no response. After waiting for another ten minutes, they exchanged concerned glances, realizing that no one was home.

"Try calling Rehan," Marc suggested to Aynaz, hoping to ascertain his whereabouts.

Aynaz dialed Rehan's number, but it went unanswered. Frowning, she remarked, "We released him from custody a few days ago. Could he have fled the country again?"

Marc shook his head. "If he's as smart as we think he is, he wouldn't risk fleeing when we have no evidence to hold him. He knows we're onto him."

Aynaz nodded, understanding the logic behind Marc's words.

Marc continued, "Call Antoine and have him track Rehan's mobile. Let's find out where he is right now."

Aynaz swiftly made the call, following Marc's instructions.

"Should we speak to Sajid about Rehan's connection?" Aynaz suggested, contemplating their next move.

Marc responded with a sarcastic tone, "You've already caused enough distress to Sajid today. It wouldn't be wise to burden him in his current state further."

Aynaz conceded, "Then what do you propose we do?"

"Did Antoine locate Rehan?" Marc inquired.

"He's working on it," Aynaz confirmed.

"Let's search Rehan's apartment while we wait for Antoine's update," Marc suggested, eager to uncover any potential clues.

Without hesitation, Aynaz broke the apartment lock, and they entered. Marc, driven by his nature, immediately began to survey the place. The apartment was new, with bright white lights illuminating the clean and tidy space. Everything seemed meticulously arranged, as if freshly cleaned. It consisted of a one-bedroom unit with an open kitchen connected to the living room.

Quietly, they moved through the apartment, searching every corner. They scoured his work desk, bedroom, nightstand, and every other area, but their efforts yielded no results. However, Marc's attention was drawn to the closet, where he noticed the same boots, he had seen at Tracey's place when they went to question her.

Approaching Marc, Aynaz remarked, "I couldn't find anything. The place is so neat and orderly; it feels like he cleaned it before leaving."

"You're right," Marc concurred, heading towards the trash cans.

Examining the contents, he focused on the dry and paper wastes. Among them, he discovered a library receipt for a late return of the book "Botany: An Introduction to Plant Biology." Suddenly, the word 'Ricin' flashed through his mind—the poison that had been used on Maysa. Ricin could be easily extracted from castor plants, or the residue of castor oil produced from castor seeds.

Momentarily stunned, Marc exclaimed, "How did we miss this book earlier? He was in our custody for almost ten days; he must have missed the deadline for returning the borrowed book from the library. That means this book was here last time we searched his apartment. How could we have missed it?"

Attempting to rationalize, Aynaz offered, "At that time, we weren't aware of the poison, so we probably saw the book but didn't consider it significant."

"You're right. Often, we observe without truly seeing what lies beneath the surface," Marc mused.

Aynaz's expression grew serious. "So, this suggests that Rehan might have been involved in the murder, and it raises suspicion about Sajid's possible involvement too."

Marc nodded thoughtfully. "Indeed. But could you please review your notes and verify the timeline of events? What time did the murder occur, and when did the delivery man spot Rehan outside the apartment?"

Aynaz retrieved her notepad and flipped through it. "According to the autopsy report, the murder took place around 5 pm. The delivery man saw Rehan outside the apartment at approximately half an hour past 5 pm, and Sajid reported the incident at a quarter to 6 pm on the 17th of March."

"That's consistent with what I recall. If Rehan committed the murder, why would he linger in the apartment for more than half an hour? Besides, I find it hard to believe that Sajid, as a father, could be capable of killing his own child," Marc confessed, his voice heavy with emotion.

"Perhaps, as you have accused me, it may be because I'm a father myself."

Aynaz pressed on, "Then how do you propose we connect the dots?"

He furrowed his brow in thought. "Could you reach out to Andre and confirm if anyone retrieved the mobile, we planted in her office?"

Aynaz compiled and reported back, "Andre is investigating. However, I suspect both Rehan and Sajid were involved in her murder."

"Let's refrain from hasty conclusions. Earlier, you were adamant about Sajid's innocence, and now you're implicating him. What about Tracey? You were convinced of her guilt earlier," Marc pointed out.

Aynaz conceded, "You're right. Initially, I didn't know about the connection between Rehan and Sajid, but now it seems plausible that Sajid enlisted Rehan's help to eliminate Maysa, perceiving her as a threat to his family."

He questioned, "But you just confirmed that he didn't know about the pregnancy, and it was you who informed them. Only Tracey was aware of the pregnancy."

She responded, "Perhaps the pregnancy news wasn't the catalyst in this narrative; there could be another overlooked trigger."

Her phone buzzed with a message from Andre, which she read aloud, "The mobile is missing from the drawer you asked me to check. Reviewing the security footage, I discovered that Tracey visited the office last night and took the mobile."

He countered, "Do you still believe she's not connected to the murder?"

"So, you suspect Tracey, Sajid, and Rehan were all involved?"

"If that is true, then I would feel very bad for Maysa. Moreover, I spotted these exact boots in Tracey's apartment," he said, gesturing towards the boots in the closet.

Another message arrived from Antoine, "I've located Rehan in Cote-des-Neiges, but he's on the move. I'll continue tracking him."

"I think I know his destination. Sajid is hospitalized in that area. We must hurry before it's too late," Marc declared, dashing towards the door.

Following him, she inquired, "How do you know he's headed there?"

"I'll explain on the way. Can you also summon Hina, Tracey, and James to the hospital?"

She nodded and trailed after him.

Chapter 18:
The Conclusion

Scene 1: In Sajid's medical room

Marc rushed into the hospital with Aynaz by his side, urgency etched on his face. They swiftly obtained Sajid's ward number from the receptionist and hurried down the corridor. Upon arrival, they found Hina and Najma already present. Relief washed over Marc's face when he noticed Rehan's absence.

Approaching Najma, Marc inquired anxiously, "How's Sajid doing?"

Najma responded with a hint of reassurance, "The doctor has confirmed he's stable, but they're keeping him under observation for a few more hours before discharge."

Sajid met Marc's gaze stoically, silently acknowledging his presence. Marc reciprocated the gesture and locked eyes with Sajid, his tone serious as he broached the sensitive topic, "I know this isn't the most appropriate time or place, but regarding your daughter's death, we need to talk. Time is of the essence."

"Have you found the killer?" Sajid's inquiry was direct, his eyes boring into Marc's.

Marc replied bluntly, "Yes!" Then he turned his face away so as not to look into his eyes directly. He said, "It was you!"

Aynaz was stunned by the accusation, conflicted by the disparity between Marc's previous assertions of Sajid's innocence and sympathy for him and this sudden accusation hurled at a vulnerable man.

Sajid's heart rate spiked on the electrocardiogram, prompting Najma to leap from her seat, grasping his hand in desperation. Tears welled in her eyes as she confronted Marc, her voice trembling with fear and anguish, "Why would you accuse my husband? I've already lost my daughter. Please, leave him alone."

Ignoring Najma's plea, Marc turns his face and looks at Sajid again, unfazed by the emotional turmoil in the room. The doctor intervened, urging everyone to leave and allow Sajid to rest, warning of the potential consequences of further agitation.

Defying the doctor's orders, Sajid interjected, his voice strained yet resolute, "No, let him stay. I want to hear why he believes this. If you've ever been a parent, you'll understand my desperation."

Reluctantly, the doctor exited the room, leaving the tension palpable in the room.

Marc kept looking at Sajid and uttered, "If this is not true, then why didn't you tell us that you knew Rehan from before? He was your daughter's friend. You knew him, and he was also a regular at your community gatherings. I think you were even friends."

The room fell into a heavy silence, punctuated only by the rapid beeping of Sajid's heart monitor. Sajid grappled with Marc's revelation, his mind racing for a response to the accusations leveled against him.

He thought to himself, "I always knew that I have to answer this question at one point or another in my life, but I never knew what to say when I am confronted with it."

Marc's accusatory glare softened momentarily as he redirected his attention to Najma, seeking clarification, "Did you know about this?"

She shook her head to say no without speaking.

Sajid's voice trembled with emotion as he responded, "Yes, I knew him before he met our daughter. But knowing someone doesn't equate to wanting harm upon your own child."

Najma recoiled, withdrawing her hand from his and covering her mouth in shock. Her eyes were filled with water and fixed on Sajid's blurry face.

Sajid's reaction was subdued this time, expecting the accusation. He remained silent, his guilt evident in his eyes.

Marc knew that Sajid was a reputed and honest man. He might have made a mistake, but he couldn't be so evil that he could have voluntarily killed his daughter. He tried to reason with him, "You thought your past would remain hidden? Trying to harm her boyfriend raises questions about your intentions. What's to stop someone from thinking you'd also go to the extent of harming your own daughter?"

Sajid replied with remorse, "I always knew the truth would surface one day. I've often pondered how I would justify my actions, but I had no answers. However, I am not involved in my daughter's death."

Aynaz intervened, sensing the escalating emotions, "We just want to know how you came to know Rehan and what kind of relation was there between you two?"

Sajid took a deep breath to compose himself and recounted, "Almost a year and a half ago, I met him in our cultural fest. He was new in Canada and didn't know a lot of people here, so he came to me, and we talked. He looked innocent at that time, so I sympathized with him and befriended him. Then, one day, he told me that he liked my daughter and wanted to marry her. In our culture, it is normal to ask the father of the girl first for her marriage, so I didn't feel offended by it; in fact, it felt more cultured. I was happy to see that someone from our young generation is still following our traditions. I explained the situation with my daughter and her live-in boyfriend to him. To this, he said that he would take care of that and would make James leave my daughter or the other way around. I thought he would try to convince her to leave James, and she might listen to him as they are of the same age. Normally, when parents tell their children not to do something, then the chance they will do increases may be as a sign of rebellion. So, I thought if someone of a similar age tried to convince her, she might listen to him. I was just being hopeful."

Sajid's emotions overwhelmed him, and he found himself succumbing to tears. "I never imagined it would come to this," he mumbled, his voice choking with grief.

Silence enveloped the room, allowing Sajid to compose himself. He wiped away his tears, drew a deep breath, and continued his narrative. "Then, one day, he asked me to transfer some money to an account, claiming it was compensation for James to leave her. In my naivety, I believed him, thinking James had agreed to exit her life for financial reasons. I didn't question the details; I was simply relieved that he would be gone."

Marc thought to himself, "It is the human tendency to believe in things easily that favor us and don't question the intentions of the person telling you that news. This is one of the main tools that con men use to con us, for example, you got a lottery, and to claim it, you just have to click here, etc. Somewhere, our brain knows that this is wrong, but our heart says to follow it. On the other hand, we question the news that is true but unfavorable to us. For example, if we don't get selected for any interview or don't get into any college, we won't believe it until we see it ourselves written in the response mail."

Sajid resumed his tale, revealing the depths of deception he had endured. "I later discovered that the money I transferred funded the truck driver who orchestrated the crash. When I confronted him, he threatened to expose my involvement, painting me as an accomplice to attempted murder. I was stunned by his duplicity. He appeared to be an ambitious, hardworking young man seeking success abroad, but a manipulative predator lay beneath the façade."

He recounted the pivotal moment of confrontation, marked by disillusionment and severed ties. "In a downtown café, I confronted him, cutting all connections thereafter. I assumed James's survival meant he had relinquished his hold over them. Only after Maysa's murder did I learn the extent of how involved he was in her life."

Sajid's gaze swept across the room, gauging their reactions. "You may doubt my account, but it is the truth. I acknowledge my naivety and misguided resentment towards James, but I bear no responsibility for either the accident or my child's murder."

Marc, though skeptical, acknowledged Sajid's explanation. "Your story is plausible. However, the driver did mention your name when we questioned him."

Sajid was shocked and thought to himself, "But I have never met that person." He countered, "Did you inquire about my appearance or voice? I've never met this person, so he wouldn't be able to recognize me."

Turning to Aynaz, Marc asked, "Can you request Antoine to create a sketch of the individual Sajid supposedly met? Antoine mentioned he had reported that he preferred a personal meeting to avoid digital traces."

Addressing Sajid again, Marc voiced his doubts. "Even if you didn't meet the driver, it doesn't absolve you of involvement. Proving otherwise will be challenging."

"I'm willing to face any consequences. I blamed myself for the accident; my emotions clouded my judgment. But I had nothing to do with my daughter's death." Sajid admitted remorsefully.

Aynaz interjected, "Did you ever inform Rehan about Tracey's feelings for James?"

"Yes, upon Hina's revelation, I thought it might sway Maysa's decisions, given her closeness to Tracey," Sajid confirmed.

"Thank you for sharing," Aynaz responded before she and Marc exited the room.

Scene 2: In-hospital lobby

Aynaz and Marc found themselves in the hospital's sterile waiting lobby, mulling over Sajid's information.

Aynaz's grin was evident as she said, "It looks like your wish came true. Sajid's innocence seems plausible."

Marc, with a furrowed brow and pursed lips, responded, "Indeed, I hoped for that outcome. Yet, until we gather concrete evidence or receive a confession, we can't exclude him from our suspect list."

Nodding, Aynaz lowered her gaze to the floor.

Marc's tone softened as he gazed at the floor, and he continued, "I just wanted that I don't lose hope in humanity. If a father tries to kill his child, then that means we are living in a world where no one can be trusted, and that raises an existential question: is it worth living in such a society? And does love exist anymore? What are we doing wrong as a society? Under no circumstances should it come to a point where we must kill anyone. The nature of our job is such that we see a lot of inhumane things every day. But I continue to do my job every day just because I believe in this society, and I know that the actions of a few shouldn't define the nature of the entire society. But this would have broken my trust as I don't want to be a part of a society where a parent can think of killing their children. I have always kept Sajid on the suspect list until proven otherwise, but to keep a father on the suspect list for the murder of her daughter was hard for me to do."

After a momentary pause, he added, "Nevertheless, personal sentiments mustn't cloud our judgment. Sajid remains a suspect until proven otherwise."

Aynaz observed the toll the case had taken on Marc, sensing his empathy for Maysa.

To divert his attention, Najma interjected, "Yes, but we've now established that Rehan was the mastermind behind all of this. So, even if Sajid was involved, it could have been due to Rehan's influence or coercion."

Sajid's response was sad. "That's even more disheartening," he muttered before falling silent.

Aynaz's phone rang, breaking the heavy atmosphere. She answered it on speaker for Marc's benefit,

"Hello, Antoine. Did you receive the sketch of the person who orchestrated James' accident?"

Antoine's voice came through the line. "No, he mentioned that he doesn't recall precisely, but he believes he could identify the person if he saw them. The individual was described as young, around 27 years old."

Marc interjected, "This confirms it wasn't Sajid who ordered James' murder. Someone was using his name to frame him."

Aynaz nodded in agreement. "Most likely, Rehan. But it's strange he hasn't arrived here yet. He was ahead of us on the way to the hospital. Why the delay?"

Marc's expression hardened. "Damn! He wasn't heading to the hospital; he was escaping. He's likely en route to the airport. Antoine, assemble a team and apprehend Rehan."

Antoine assured him, "Understood, Sir. I'll mobilize immediately. My apologies for jumping to conclusions too hastily. I've also briefed Marshall on the situation."

He ended the call, and the room fell into a tense silence.

Scene 3: James and Tracey's entry

Aynaz noticed Tracey and James standing in the ward with Sajid. Marc and Aynaz entered the room.

With a stern voice, Marc addressed Tracey, "The only person who gained anything from her death is you."

Tracey glanced at James before returning her gaze to Marc. "You're mistaken, Sir. James and I are just friends. We're both hurting and found solace in each other's company."

Interrupting, Aynaz interjected, "Hina, Sajid, Najma, and Roohi are all grieving. Why seek solace only with James?"

Although tempted to argue further, Tracey remained silent, realizing they were aware of her feelings for James.

James spoke up, "Tracey and I are simply supporting each other through this difficult time. Maysa's death has nothing to do with our friendship."

Marc's tone remained firm. "Considering you may not be aware of her true feelings; she had feelings for you all along."

Taken aback, James turned to Tracey, seeking confirmation. "Is this true?"

Tracey nodded. "Yes, I liked you. I intended for her to see us together the day you met Maysa so I could confess, but events unfolded differently."

"Why didn't you say anything afterward? Did you have a hand in her death?" James inquired.

Tracey's defensive tone sliced through the tense air, her voice rising. "I could never even think of doing that to her. Maysa was like an angel to me. How could I shatter her heart by revealing the truth? I chose silence."

Aynaz observed Tracey's reaction while Marc maintained his stern demeanor. "We know that you were aware of her pregnancy and that you took her phone from her office yesterday. These actions imply you're concealing something."

The room fell into shocked silence as everyone's attention turned to Tracey, who began to cry but offered no explanation.

Aynaz intervened firmly, "Refusing to speak the truth won't help you."

With a trembling voice, Tracey began, "I don't know where to begin. I've kept this buried deep within me. Maysa and Hina were my saviors, but I always felt indebted, like a charity case. I never spoke of my past, fearing judgment and labeling."

With a pause and wiping her tears, she continued with a clear voice, "I love her and Hina from the bottom of my heart. What they did for me was more than anyone could ever ask for; they returned my life to me, and I was able to face society with them, but deep down inside, I felt that they were my friend only out of pity. I felt that I was a charity work for them. After people come to know about my past, they all look at me with pity. I just wanted her to have a normal family, a loving dad, a loving sister, a normal life, a loving boyfriend, and a successful career. So, when I used to see her not appreciating what she had got, it made me jealous and annoyed as God has given her everything, but she doesn't appreciate it. On the other hand, I wanted it so badly, but I could never have it. She used to fight with her father, James, and even Hina and me. It just made me sad seeing people not appreciating what god has given them, and they don't value their life."

Her voice started to brittle, "When she told me that she was pregnant, it made me feel so happy for her that I almost started to rejoice. But then she told me that the baby was Rehan's. I was speechless for two minutes, and I got so angry with her, as I felt that she was throwing everything away, including her beautiful family. I blasted her with a long text reply, in which I even said that I truly regret sending her the message that I wish she would never have come into my life. I didn't mean that I was just so sad and angry at her, as she was going to lose a lovely man like James just because she was having some trouble in her life, so she turned to a random guy and got intimate with him."

The revelation stunned everyone, especially Marc and Aynaz, who had presumed James was the father.

She continued, "I just thought if you would have read that message, then you would have thought that I was behind the murder. Also, I didn't want anyone to know that she was pregnant with someone else's baby, and that would hamper her image. I never wanted bad for her, and after her death, I felt bad for James, and this brought me closer to him. Yes, I like him, but I loved her even more. I wouldn't have done anything to hurt her, and that's why I never told her about James when I realized they were happy together."

Aynaz pressed, "Did Rehan attempt to sway you?"

Tracy divulged, "Yes, about six months ago, Rehan approached me, suggesting I help him break up James and Maysa so he could pursue her while I could pursue James. I refused, stating both James and Maysa held equal importance to me, if not more for her. Rehan attempted to coerce me by threatening to disclose my feelings for James to Maysa, but I had nothing to hide, so his threats held no sway. I did inform her about Rehan's intentions and his threat, but she seemed content with their friendship, and given her struggles with depression and anxiety, I believed Rehan could be a positive influence. Looking back, I regret not being more forthright with her."

Marc interjected, incredulous, "Do you have any evidence to support your claims? We found no such conversations on Maysa's phone."

Tracy admitted, "I realized after taking her phone from her office yesterday that she had deleted those messages, but I retained copies of them on my phone. Additionally, you'll find Rehan's earlier messages and his threatening texts on my phone. Initially, with Rehan's arrest, I hesitated to reveal this, not wanting to tarnish her reputation posthumously."

Marc instructed, "Aynaz, seize Tracy's phone. These messages could bolster our case against Rehan if she is telling the truth."

Perplexed, Aynaz questioned, "But why would Rehan harm her if he was the father of her child?"

Hina intervened, embracing Tracy for support. Marc and Aynaz exited the room silently, leaving Tracy and Hina to their thoughts.

Chapter 19:
We need a confession!

Aynaz and Marc returned to the police station, accompanied by Rehan, whom Antoine had apprehended at the airport just before his departure to India.

Aynaz contemplated their next steps. "How do you propose we approach the interrogation?"

Marc considered their options carefully. "Given Rehan's cunning nature, we need to proceed cautiously."

Aynaz acknowledged the challenges. "Our strongest evidence lies in the testimony of the driver involved in the attempted murder of James. However, this implicates Rehan in the attack on James, not necessarily Maysa's murder."

"But let's not overlook the delivery person who identified Rehan on the day of the murder," Marc reminded her. "We also have the library receipt indicating Rehan's interest in botany, potentially linking him to the drug administered to Maysa. And now, there are the threatening messages he sent to Tracey."

"We may have a compelling case," Marc continued, "but extracting the truth from Rehan will require a strategic approach aimed at securing a confession."

After a moment of reflection, Marc voiced a lingering

question. "Considering Maysa's apparent happiness with James, why would she engage in a relationship with Rehan?"

Aynaz gazed out the window, her tone resigned. "How was she supposed to know what was right for her? There was a boyfriend who was jealous and possessive of her. There was her father, who didn't approve of her boyfriend and didn't accept him instead of being proud of her professional achievements. Then, there was a younger sibling who looked up to her and whom she wouldn't want to make the same mistakes she had. There were her friends who were getting jealous of her success and hiding things from her. In such vulnerability, Rehan's attention may have appeared as an escape from all these issues in her life, leading her to succumb to his manipulation. It's a situation where anyone could have fallen prey."

Aynaz turned to Marc, her voice laden with contemplation. "She couldn't discern what was truly best for her at that moment. Perhaps she saw Rehan as the solution to her myriad troubles. Sajid would have welcomed her back with open arms. James's harassment would have ceased, and perhaps her friends would have found solace in her happiness."

Marc continued driving, allowing Najma's thoughts to flow uninterrupted.

As they neared their destination, Marc interjected, "I comprehend your perspective. It's plausible that Maysa's encounter with Rehan stemmed from a desire for escape. However, we must remember that the interrogation process begins long before the actual questioning. In Maysa's case, we may need to approach Rehan under the assumption of manipulation or coercion to elicit a confession. Considering her affection for James, other evidence alone might not suffice. Our line of questioning should reflect this."

"Understood, Captain. I'll follow your lead," Aynaz affirmed.

*****

Rehan sat in the interrogation room, his expression unreadable as Marc and Aynaz entered.

Aynaz settled into a chair in the corner, a hint of familiarity in her tone. "Feels like deja vu, doesn't it?"

Marc placed a thick file on the table opposite Rehan. "This time, it's a bit more serious," he remarked dryly.

Rehan remained silent; his gaze fixed on the file.

Marc's tone shifted to a deeper register as he leaned forward, resting his hand on the file. "Before we proceed, you should know you're being arrested for double homicide and attempted murder. You have the right to request a lawyer. If you can't afford one, the state will provide it."

He continued, listing the damning evidence against Rehan. "We know you plotted to kill James last year in May, and we have proof for that. We know that on the day Maysa was killed, you were present in her apartment and have proof of that as well. We know that Maysa was pregnant with your child and have proof of that as well. We know you borrowed the books that teach how to make the poison that was used to kill her and have proof for that. We know that you were trying to flee from here when we strictly instructed you to inform us if you are leaving the town, let alone the country. Do you have anything to say against these charges?"

Rehan's eyes flickered over the file, absorbing the weight of the accusations.

Marc observed Rehan's lack of reaction and pressed on, "If you truly cared for her, why did you commit such a heinous act?"

Rehan's gaze met Marc's, but he remained silent.

Marc's tone hardened as he continued, "You raped and murdered her, knowing she was carrying your child. How do you justify such cruelty?"

"I won't speak without my lawyer present," Rehan stated firmly.

Marc nodded, understanding the protocol. "You have the right to legal representation. We'll arrange for your lawyer."

As Marc and Aynaz exited the room, Antoine entered and offered Rehan a phone. "You're entitled to one call," he said.

Rehan dialed his lawyer's number, only to discover the lawyer was unavailable.

Antoine's smirk conveyed the situation. "Seems luck isn't on your side. You can request a government-appointed lawyer, but it's Saturday evening. You'll be in custody until Monday, during which time we can question you."

Antoine left the room, maintaining his composure. Rehan's eyes remained fixed on the file before him.

No one entered the interrogation room for another two hours.

Rehan sat alone, contemplating what to say to Marc upon his

return, but Marc never appeared. Instead, an attendant silently placed a glass of water on the table and left without a word.

Marc and Aynaz observed Rehan through a one-way look-through glass window. They noticed him starting to doze off, prompting them to send another attendant to place a glass of water and wake him up.

Throughout the night, they repeated this cycle, denying Rehan proper sleep.

*****

Rehan wasn't able to sleep the entire night, and around 7 am on Sunday, Aynaz entered the room alone, carrying two cups of coffee. She placed one cup in front of Rehan and took a sip from the other.

"You look tired," she said with a fake smile. "Have some coffee."

Despite his frustration from the previous night, Rehan attempted to remain composed. "I appreciate the gesture, but I'm not interested."

Aynaz persisted, "I'm just trying to help you feel more alert for our discussion. Are you hungry? I could get you something to eat."

Though Rehan's stomach growled in protest after fifteen hours without proper food, he refrained from expressing his hunger.

"Suit yourself," Aynaz shrugged, taking the coffee with her as she left the room.

Throughout the next two hours, individuals entered the room at regular intervals, preventing Rehan from resting or sleeping.

At 9 am on Sunday morning, Marc entered alone, empty-handed this time.

Looking at Marc, Rehan's frustration boiled over, and said, "Your tactics won't work on me. I won't say anything without my lawyer present."

To this, Marc rose silently from his seat and exited the room without uttering a word.

An hour later, they delivered food and coffee once more, and this time, hunger overpowered his reluctance, compelling him to partake. As he ate and drank, a sense of refreshment and alertness washed over him.

Marc and Aynaz returned to the room shortly after repeating their previous statements and charges. Yet, he remained steadfast, unmoved by their efforts, prompting their departure once more.

Feeling revitalized after consuming coffee, sleep eluded him. Instead, he settled into the chair, conserving his energy, preparing for the long night ahead, and anticipating consulting his lawyer come Monday morning.

In the adjoining room, where Marc and Aynaz observed him, Aynaz voiced her concern, "Why did you leave the file folder in front of him? Half of the pages in that file are for another case. What if he opened it and saw what's inside?"

He calmly replies, "We are more influenced by our

surroundings than we realize. That file will act as a catalyst for him to remind him of all the horrible things he has done. He had the entire night, and he kept quiet for the whole night, which means he was talking to himself and thinking about something or the other in his mind. This file would have focused his thoughts on Maysa or the things he had done to her. This was a gamble, and I never knew if he would open it or not, but even if he would have opened it, then we would have just removed the file from the room."

After a pause, he continued, "Still wondering why it was necessary?"

She nodded.

"Do you know what the main reason for people to confess their crime is?"

She said, "Because of the fear that they will be convicted even for a longer time if they didn't."

He replied, "Well, partly yes, fear is one major factor, but it is not just fear; it is also guilt. The guilt of doing something that will change their life forever and that they can't now undo. So, the only path they can take now is to confess their crime as they see no other paths for mercy."

She was amazed by the logic behind just putting a file in that room and said, "So, it's true everything that happens in that room happens for a reason, and everything factors towards interrogation."

He smiled while parting his wisdom with someone.

After twenty-four hours of his arrest at 7 pm on Sunday, Marc and Aynaz entered the room once more. Rehan hadn't had any sleep in the last thirty-six hours. He had only one meal in the last twenty-four hours and was in the same small interrogation room for the past twenty-four hours with that file still placed in front of him. He was trying to hold up, but he looked much less determined now than he was twenty-four hours ago.

Aynaz positioned herself in a corner, her tone dripping with sarcasm. "Monsieur, Looking sharp!"

Suddenly aware of his vulnerability, Rehan resolved to remain cautious and not allow himself to be manipulated. He corrected his posture by sitting up straight.

Sitting opposite to him, Marc cut straight to the point. "Why did you rape her?"

Rehan remained silent.

"Do you honestly believe you'll get away with it? We know it was you, and we have sufficient evidence to charge you. We let you go once, but that won't happen again. You may have deceived us with your charming words before, but not this time. You're facing a minimum sentence of life imprisonment."

Even in his current state, Rehan remained composed and silent.

Marc exploded in anger. "Are you waiting for your lawyer? Do you think he can save you from the mess you've made? You're already in a deep hole, and there's no escape. Do you honestly believe you can get away with raping and killing a girl?"

Rehan's composure shattered this time, and he retorted, "I didn't rape her! I loved her."

They realize that he didn't oppose the accusation of murder, but he did for rape.

Interrupting with a calm voice, Aynaz interjected, "Alright, we'll entertain that notion. But you need to tell us what happened if you want any chance of help."

Once again, Rehan fell silent.

Aynaz persisted, "She was a bright, promising young woman. Why would you want to destroy her? She was from your country, your religion. Why rape and kill her? Where was your empathy?"

Marc's glare intensified, thickening the tension in the room.

Avoiding eye contact, Rehan muttered, "I never raped her. And if she was as happy and successful as you claim, why was she seeking solace with me? Why was she taking antidepressants?"

Marc detected guilt in Rehan's eyes. "Did you love her?"

Meeting Marc's gaze, Rehan replied, "Yes, with all my heart."

With a stern tone, Marc pressed, "Then why did you rape her?"

Frustration laced Rehan's voice. "I didn't rape her! We had consensual sex."

Aynaz asked with a softer tone, "Can you explain then what happened?"

With a small pause and soft voice, he continued, "I loved her, but she didn't love me back the way I did. She used to feel happy with me and shared all her troubles with me. I never took advantage of her, even when I got the chance, and she was very comfortable around me. Whenever she fought with James or had a disagreement in the office or a quarrel with Sajid, she used to turn to me to talk. She felt happy with me."

Aynaz asked, "How did you feel?"

He continued, "I felt complete with her as if she was giving me purpose in being alive. The first time I saw her, I just felt attracted to her and I asked for her hand from her father like any decent person would do. But then I found out that she was dating someone else. At that point, I thought I would forget about her and move on with my life, but then I came to know that Sajid was against her relationship and saw an opportunity to pursue her. At that time, my feelings were not that strong, and I just wanted to try."

After a pause, he continued, "But the more I learned about her, the crazier I got for her. I just wanted James to vanish from her life. Also, I wanted to impress Sajid so that she would have been all mine when James was gone, and Sajid wouldn't mind. So, I orchestrated his accident in a way that it wouldn't trace back to us. I was sure that, because of the amount of hate Sajid had for James, he wouldn't mind if he was gone from this world. But he survived."

"After that, I tried to leave them alone in their life, but then I noticed that James' behavior towards her had changed considerably. He started to follow her, doubt her, blame her for things she hadn't even done, fight with her on small things, and mistreat her. At this point, I just wanted to help her realize that she could be happy without him. So, I befriended her, and since she needed someone on her side, just by listening to her, we easily grew closer."

"We talked for hours," he began, his tone tinged with anger, "and she shared all her troubles, insecurities, and self-doubts with me. We connected so deeply that she even stopped taking her antidepressants at one point. But then James found out about us. Although we hadn't done anything wrong, his jealousy and insecurity drove him to demand she stop talking to me. And she did, for a while."

His anger simmered as he continued, "I wanted to lash out at him, to make him pay for interfering, but I knew it would only push her away. So, I waited, biding my time until she reached out to me again. And she did, unable to resist the connection between us. I had flirted with her from the start, but she never took it seriously."

Softening his tone, he added, "Then, one day, I offered her a way out. I proposed, promising to help her escape her misery. Her father would have understood, and she could have left her abusive boyfriend behind. But she refused me, claiming she still loved him. I was furious. How could she choose to stay with someone who made her suffer, rejecting the one offering her a chance at happiness?"

He paused, his thoughts weighing heavily on him. Marc and Aynaz remained silent, allowing him to continue.

"One day, after a particularly heated argument with James, she sought refuge with me," he recounted. "She had achieved a major client in office and wanted to share that moment with James, but James saw it as a personal affront, accusing her of flaunting her achievements. He's a spiteful man. They fought, and she fled to me, unable to turn to her parents, who would have urged her to leave James for good. I comforted her and reassured her of our support no matter what. She couldn't control her feelings for me that night, and we got intimate. I didn't force her or drug her or threaten her; it was consensual."

He fell into a tense silence. After a while, Marc's voice pierced the quiet, laden with accusation. "If everything was going so well for you, why did you kill her?"

His frustration spilled out. "I couldn't understand her. Even after sleeping with me, she insisted on staying with James, claiming she still loved him. I became desperate, unable to imagine life without her. I pursued her relentlessly, even resorting to threats of exposing our affair to James. But she remained steadfast, refusing to leave him for me. I turned to Tracey, urging her to intervene with James, but she refused."

His voice softened, a hint of vulnerability creeping in, "Then one day she told me that she was pregnant with my baby, and I got so happy by that news that I just wanted to climb a mountain and shout it out to everyone. But then she crushed my happiness by telling me that she was going to get an abortion, and it was a mistake that she doesn't want to remember."

His tone grew brittle. "From then on, she distanced herself, cutting off communication. I felt utterly alone."

As he continued, a tear escaped his eye, his voice cracking with emotion. "I never wanted to harm her. I loved her deeply; all I wanted was to be with her. The thought of her aborting our child was unbearable. I tried to reason with her, to console her, but she remained resolute – she would never marry me, even if I were the last man on earth."

With a mixture of tears and anger, he confessed, "I saw no other option but to end her life. I couldn't bear the thought of her living without me, knowing she had killed our child. Poison seemed the simplest method. I waited for an opportunity when James would be away, then slipped into her apartment and tainted her tea."

After a short pause, he continued, "Before I administered the fatal dose, I pleaded with her one last time. I asked her if she would take me and love me the way I love her. I tried to convince her that her life would be sorted. We could raise our children in love and happiness. And I tried to reason with her that her parents would be happy with her also, and all her problems would be gone."

He then continued with heavy breathing and low pitch voice, "But she refused, and I had no choice," and he then burst into tears sitting opposite Marc in that interrogation room.

Epilogue

Picking up his order of black coffee and Montreal bagels from his favorite cafe, Marc said, "So, Rehan is facing double homicide charges and one attempt to murder charges."

Aynaz nodded without saying anything as she waited for her French vanilla.

"Mr. Sajid will also face a case for the attempt to murder James, but in my opinion, he has a strong alibi, and it should be easy for him to prove innocence. Najma is still deeply hurt from the death of her child and the involvement of her husband with Rehan, but she has focused herself on raising her younger child." Marc continued.

Aynaz replied, "I have heard Hina, James, and Tracey have continued with their lives separately but continue to be friends."

After a pause, as she looked at the floor, she asked, "Do you really think Rehan was solely responsible for Maysa's death?"

Marc looked at Aynaz, staring at the floor, and replied, "Absolutely not; everyone to some extent is responsible here. Had there been a loving boyfriend, things would have been different. Had there been understanding parents, things would have been been different. Had there been caring friends, things would have been different for Maysa."

Continued with a softer tone, "We should always try to foster a caring environment for our loved ones lest other people take advantage of them or us."

As the waiter called for Marc's and Aynaz's orders, his chain of thoughts broke.

Aynaz, picking up her French vanilla, says cheeringly, "Let's head out to solve another Montreal mystery, but this time, let's do it in the first 7 days of the crime."